Through Misadventures Lurks

LIFE
and
DEATH

STORIES

Tristan Armstrong

This is a work of fiction. All of the characters, names, incidents,
organizations, and dialogue in this novel are either the
products of the author's imagination or are used fictitiously.

Archway Publishing books may be ordered
through booksellers or by contacting:

Archway Publishing
1663 Liberty Drive
Bloomington, IN 47403
www.archwaypublishing.com
1 (888) 242-5904

Because of the dynamic nature of the Internet, any web
addresses or links contained in this book may have changed
since publication and may no longer be valid. The views
expressed in this work are solely those of the author and do
not necessarily reflect the views of the publisher, and the
publisher hereby disclaims any responsibility for them.

Any people depicted in stock imagery provided
by Thinkstock are models, and such images are
being used for illustrative purposes only.
Certain stock imagery © Thinkstock.

ISBN: 978-1-4808-5123-8 (sc)
ISBN: 978-1-4808-5122-1 (e)

Library of Congress Control Number: 2017953473

Print information available on the last page.

Archway Publishing rev. date: 08/29/2017

Special thanks for this publication must go to Terry Hill for developmental editing along with support and encouragement. Besides being a NASA engineer, Terry is an author in his own right with his series In the Days of Humans and is duly acknowledged in the Amazon best-selling Future Chronicles anthology series.

Thanks also go to my wife, Christina, who has stood by me in my emotional highs and lows when writing and rewriting this manuscript.

And a thank-you to Cherrie, an art associate, for her display at Gallery La Crosse, for her decorated switch covers, which gave me the idea to use them in juxtapositions and stylize them for background material. I've used them in some of my gallery displays and well as on my artist website. I have her full endorsement.

CONTENTS

A Wayward Man 1

Correspondence 9

Expectations 18

Jason's Glitch 29

The Tale of Crispinus and Hilarinus 39

Brother Michael and Kola... 88

Missed Detail.. 127

My Queen..139

Slip Sliding Away 146

Which Ship?..156

About the Author 169

A WAYWARD MAN

Richard Wellingham's assignment was to be a pretentious little man contriving to overthrow the reigning kabaka, Sir Edward Mutessa II. The target of the covert operation was Undersecretary M. Mbogo, who was scheduled to deliver a grand-opening speech for Medical Co-op, a new missionary and medical establishment, in Pakwach, Uganda, in East Africa. Undersecretary Mbogo had been under surveillance and the collected information wasn't good. There was growing evidence that he was in the center of a plot to overthrow Sir Edward in a military coup. This was exactly what the State Department was working to prevent, with as little fuss or commotion as possible. Sir Edward Mutessa II was the great-great-grandson of Mwanga, who, with Captain Lugard, played a key role in the statehood of Uganda in its early colonial days. The State Department had sanctioned the hit of M. Mbogo as a favor to the British Foreign Office, which for political reasons had to appear clean of the operation. How or why the British Foreign Office had gotten mixed up in the Uganda situation was anybody's guess. And this was where Richard came in.

Railroad car 7 gently swayed in the early morning as it crept northward, away from the teeming Kenyan city of Nairobi. Richard adjusted his stocky frame and lifted his sleep-filled eyes to the window of the car. Now and then, a white building of one size or another would glide slowly by. He wondered if life in general wasn't some big accident waiting to happen, and he wondered if he really wanted to stay in his present position. Hell, he didn't even want to stay in the department or any facet thereof. A complete change in venue might do him a world of good.

Awakened again from his reverie, Richard glanced over at the passenger seated next to him. She too was dozing, the sun intermittently breaking in on her. Her paper had slipped from her lap. She was attractive with a short, distinct nose, arched eyebrows, and dark hair. Her elegant features were all too like those of another young woman in his past, from what seemed so long ago. As with most naturally beautiful women, it was impossible to tell her age, and besides, he was a poor judge of age anyway. She was truly beautiful. Her long legs were stretched out in slumber, as his had been just moments before.

A mismatched trestle jarred Richard from his thoughts. He tapped his left side, the familiar hard lump reassuring him the Mauser was still nestled in the shoulder harness underneath his jacket. *Damn, it's 1965! Thirty-two years old and still chasing across the country, running down unsavory individuals who need removing from life's stage,* Richard thought. *Being like other real people, raising a family with a steady nine-to-five job and having weekends off just isn't to be my lot in life. Or is it?*

The sound of footsteps coming down the aisle marked the progress of the porter. Once abreast of Richard's row of seats, he looked Richard's way, garnered Richard's sight, albeit briefly, and then ambled on to the next car.

That was a bit odd! Richard thought.

He returned to his train of thought. "Maybe I'm not real. Wouldn't that be a bitch?" Richard said quietly to himself.

"What?" asked the female passenger seated next to him.

"Oh, I'm sorry. Did I wake you? If I did, I didn't mean to. I was just thinking out loud, I guess. I apologize, Miss ... Miss ..." Richard said as he leaned over and picked up her fallen newspaper.

"Miss Elizabeth Ann Howe, and thank you," Elizabeth replied, taking the paper from his hand. "How many miles have we traveled so far, or should I say kilometers, as this country is, I believe, on the metric system?"

"We're still in Kenya, a little over halfway between Nairobi and Naivasha—about fifty kilometers out of Naivasha, which is our next stop. In answer to your question, I believe we've come about seventy klicks or kilometers. Out of curiosity, why are you on this train, and where are you headed?"

"I'm a missionary based out of Atlanta, Georgia. I'm on my way to Pakwach in Uganda. This is my first assignment," she replied.

"By any remote chance, are you headed for the new Medical Co-op opening?"

"Why yes. I'm surprised you would know anything about it. That's my destination, and I must tell you, I'm pretty excited about it."

Looking at her, he thought, *this could be interesting.* "I'm a journalist," he volunteered. "I'm to do a cover story on the grand opening of the medical site."

The railroad car lurched as it traversed another mismatched railroad trestle. An announcement came over the public-address system, first in French and then in English. "May I have your attention, please. The train will be stopping in Naivasha and then in Eldoret before leaving Kenya. There will be a one-hour delay in Naivasha and an almost two-hour delay in Eldoret while the train switches engines. You may leave the car in each case, but please be aware of departure times."

"Can I buy you something to eat at our next stop?" Richard asked. *She should make a good ally and cover. She seems to be as innocent and honest as the day is long. Most likely what she said about herself is true.* Questioning what people told him was in his nature, based on years of experience in the field. This time, however, he had little doubt she was telling the truth.

"I'm not very hungry, but I could use a soda if you would be so kind."

"You've got it," he replied, almost saying *babe* before he stopped himself.

An awkward silence followed, broken only by the repetitive clanking of the wheels on the trestle joints. Richard scanned the car while looking for any potential intruders who could possibly interfere with his plans.

They all looked harmless, the basic mix of fellow travelers and locals. No one seemed to be appraising him or even paying any attention.

Suddenly, the railroad car violently heaved sideways, as if thrown by an angry child. Screeching of metal on metal, popping and breaking of glass, and splintering wood assailed his ears. Instinctively, he rolled to the floor, away from the windows, pulling Elizabeth down with him. In the cacophony of sounds and screams, a man came toward Richard with a startled look on his face.

No, only the head of the man was approaching!

"Good God!" Movement in Richard's periphery drew his attention, revealing a decapitated body hunched over in its seat and rhythmically spurting blood.

Someone screamed again, accompanied by a long wail. The railroad car continued in its sideways movement with glass shattering, metal wrenching, and seats breaking loose. Richard lay twisted on the floor between the seats, and something was jabbing into the small of his back, causing pain. The seat across the aisle from where he and Elizabeth were sitting had sheared loose and thrust itself up against him. He was still holding on to Elizabeth's arm. She gave a soft whimper as he let go of her. She was crumpled up around his legs and shaking but looked to be all right. Reaching behind to move the seat was fruitless; it was jammed, pinning him in place. A broken branch protruded from the back of the impaled head above them, still dripping blood.

"Lie still, and don't look up," Richard commanded.

The din started to subside. No one moved. Despite the intense pain, Richard reached up and shoved the broken branch with the man's head onto the seat right above them. It needed to be relatively out of sight before Elizabeth saw it; there were some things women should never have to see. Even he felt a little nauseous at the sight. He was no stranger to death, but this had just about topped everything he'd seen. A shot of pain went through his lower back and legs as he tried to sit and brush the broken glass off himself, but that was not to be. Unable to stand or straighten out, he rolled over onto his side.

"Oh shit. Oh shit. This isn't good," Richard whispered, trying to maintain his composure. His mouth and throat felt dry. He was sweating. "Elizabeth, are you hurt? Can you move?"

"I think I'm okay. Just shaken," she replied. "Thank you. You probably saved my life."

"Listen. You've got to help me now. It's painful for me to move. See how many others are hurt and get some help."

Things would quickly become even more complicated if anyone found the gun on him, so while she was away and distracted, he jammed it into some broken seat boards along with its harness. This just left some straps on his chest, which could be explained away if needed.

There was another explosion, and more broken glass went flying. A board broke through what remained of the folding doors, leading into the car's compartment.

"How many are hurt?" a voice in English called through the now-opened door. A dark-skinned military man in a scuffed uniform, followed by a porter, the same one as earlier, came through the opening. The porter now had a cut above his right eye and was holding a towel to his head.

"Anyone killed?" the soldier asked, as if the dead could respond.

"One killed, I believe, and it's painful ... for me ... to move. I took a blow to the back!" Richard responded, moaning between words.

"Lay still. We have doctors coming," the soldier said as he leaned over. "A medical station is being set up toward the back of the train. Medical evacuation teams are going to be flying the severely injured out."

The officer turned, said a few hushed words to the porter, and abruptly left, leaving the porter standing there.

"I've got to make a phone call," Richard said, looking up at the porter.

"Did you lose your gun?" the porter asked, looking down at him. "I had to wait until the officer left to say anything. It's okay, Richard; I'm supposed to cover for you, in case a 'negative' slipped in on the train that we might have missed."

Richard sighed with relief. "It's just above my head, jammed into some broken wood. Get rid of it for me, will you?"

"Don't worry. It'll disappear," the porter replied.

"What the hell happened anyway?"

"Well, as you probably guessed, the tracks were not in that good of shape to begin with. However, it looks like somebody helped things along by pulling out a trestle. I don't think we were the object of their attention, though. Someone or some group must have had a beef with the railroad. It wasn't a professional job. Tools are all over the place."

"Are we the only team out?" Richard asked. "Was all this effort really necessary and that important?"

"I can't answer that, because I honestly don't know what the whole picture was or is."

"I understand because, obviously, I don't either. Look, I sent my young traveling friend to get help and to see if she could help others. Before she returns, I need to ask a favor of you. She is a complete novice, so ... could you see to it that she gets to her destination? It's the same as ours. For obvious reasons, she has no knowledge of our affairs. She is a missionary and I planned on using her as part of my cover as a journalist." After another stab of pain shot through him, leaving him gasping. "Maybe ... you should step in and finish the job. You use her for cover!"

Before the porter could reply, Elizabeth appeared through the opening, followed by medical personnel bearing a litter. As medical staff gently lifted Richard onto the stretcher, the porter leaned in and gave Richard a thumbs-up.

As the porter left, Elizabeth shot Richard a quizzical look.

Richard, catching her glance, said between moans of pain as he was carried out, "Its nothing, Elizabeth, absolutely nothing. You'll be all right."

Before giving in to a shot of morphine just administered, he thought, *maybe this is the accident that will change my life forever.*

CORRESPONDENCE

A lex turned sixty-two on October 25. He sat alone in his rocker, reading the evening paper. About halfway down the page in the personal column, an advertisement caught his eye:

> Adult female desires pen pal.
> Hobbies include reading, writing,
> and chess. Reply to box 2552,
> Ad 4774.

Alex had long since drifted into the habit of not talking to anyone but his empty surroundings. "I wonder," he said quietly. "Agnes has been gone now for two years, and I played some chess in my time. It might be worthwhile to reply to this one."

Alex lived in a small, second-floor flat overlooking Cleveland Avenue in a suburb of Chicago, Illinois. The fall chill was creeping in, so he couldn't take as many walks as he once did.

Dear ad 4774,

I am a single male, sixty-two years of age,
and enjoy chess.

Sincerely,
Alex Stanislav

"There, that should do it. Anyway, it beats reading
laundry lists. Now, to put it in the mail and see what
happens."

As the electric coffeepot perked in the late morning,
Alex went to check his mail. It was Friday, and
hopefully there would be a reply from ad 4774 before
the weekend. Boredom and nervousness set in for want
of activity. Still agile for his age, Alex made the walk to
the mailbox in no time, and there, sure enough, was
a small envelope. He just about jumped for glee, but
the other neighbors were coming for their mail and
would probably wonder about an old man jumping up
and down. With long, quick strides, he returned to his
apartment and then made a little jump. A letter in one
hand and a cup of coffee in the other, he sat at the
kitchen table and began to read.

Dear Alex,

Thank you for your response. For some
reason, you were my choice out of five
replies. So, "number one," I suggest we

get to know each other over chess through correspondence. My opening move—white, king's pawn, one (e2-e3).

Sincerely,
Silvia Rudanski

"How about that … Now to find the chessboard. I'll beat the pants off her." He chuckled. "There's still life in the old boy yet!"

Elated at having an objective for the weekend, he went rummaging through the closet for an old chess set that he and Agnes used to play with. There at the very bottom, underneath a pile of shoe boxes filled with records, rested the chess pieces and board. The set was covered with much dust and lint, but there it was. It was beautiful.

"Now, where to set up? Ah, yes … on the end table of course."

Clouds of dust filled the air as he brushed off the set, humming to himself as he did so. The upcoming weekend did not seem so long now. After setting up and placing her move as directed, he studied the board and placed his move.

Dear Silvia,

Black, king's knight to black king's bishop, two (g8-f6). I'm most happy to engage you in a game. As you see, I'm giving you my countermove. My opening should not

distress you too much. I think you'll find
me to be quite an adversary.

Sincerely,
Number One

Hopping a bus early Monday morning, Alex took
his response to the main post office so that Silvia would
receive it as soon as possible. There was a skip in his
step and a smile on his face.

I'll be gentle with her, he thought on leaving the
post office. Speaking to no one in particular, he said,
"Well, maybe not. I'll beat her at this game and then ...
who knows? I wonder what she looks like. I wonder if
we will ever meet, and if we do, then what?"

* * * * *

Dear Number One:

White, king's knight to king's bishop,
two (g1-f3). I think your opening is very
cautious. I respect that. However, you'll
never beat me. I'll bet you're cautious in
life too.

Enclosed is a picture of myself.

Sincerely,
Silvia

In front of his chess set, Alex sat reading her
letter. The late-afternoon sun was filtering in past the

partially closed drapes, and a single reading lamp was turned on to wash away the shadows. First one way and then another, he placed her picture to best suit his view while planning his next move.

"Ah, Silvia ... you are a beauty, aren't you? So, you think I'm cautious, huh? Wait till my queen sweeps down on you, trailing her bishops."

He debated with himself as to what it would be like to meet Silvia, to talk to her in person, or to listen to her conversation across a breakfast table.

Dear Silvia,

Hi again from Chicago. Black queen's pawn, two (d7-d5). You will soon feel the trap. I hope you can stand the pressure.

Do you get out very much? I try to take as many walks as possible. One more question: Do you ever come through Chicago on your travels?

Your picture was very much appreciated, thank you. Enclosed is a picture of myself leaning against a tree in front of my apartment building. The one on the right is me, and the green one on the left is the tree. I thought I'd tell you so there is no confusion. I'm a bit tall.

Sincerely,
Number One

Dear Alex,

Thank you for your picture and your latest
chess move. You look very handsome parked
next to the tree, and, judging from the other
objects in the picture, you're not that tall.
What's this pressure you're talking about?
You're not even close to capturing my king.
My move—white, queen's knight to queen's
bishop, two (b1-c3). Don't get nervous now.

With love,
Silvia

Alex sat back in his chair, holding her latest letter in
his hand. *Oh my! She signed "with love" ... how about
that,* he thought. *Would she ever come to Chicago? I
can win, but would winning be the best move?*

If she ever were to come to Chicago and they spent
some time together, then what? Afterward, would they
continue their correspondence? Would they become
more than just friends ... lovers? Would there be
a proposal at some point, at his age? There were no
obvious answers. Regardless of the questions raised, he
did want to see her in person, and perhaps she would
want to see him as well.

Dear Silvia,

My move—black, king's pawn, one (e7-e6).
My bishop is now free to move out—things
just got serious. Speaking of moving, are
you ever free to leave Eton? Illinois is
not that big of a state; we're not that far

away from each other. We could be seated together pondering our next move.

With the warmest regards,
Alex

Two weeks passed, and still no letter from Silvia. Daily routines were becoming just that. In another week on Friday, it would be their two-month anniversary of corresponding over chess. Had he come on too strong? Yet the last letter of hers was signed "with love." *Could she be sick?* he wondered. Probably not. If she were, he felt reasonably sure she would have said something in one of her last letters. Hopefully she was still alive and no accident had befallen her.

Late that afternoon, there was a rap at the door, followed by an unfamiliar female voice. "Alex, are you home? If so, your bishop is going to get nailed!"

He jumped up from his chair, sending the reading lamp tumbling end over end in the process. He called out, "Just a minute!"

A last-minute look around confirmed that both he and the apartment were a mess. It was not the ideal situation for them to meet, but she had forced his next move. He opened the door and stood there feeling completely off guard and naked.

"Well, are you just going to stand there, or are you going to let me in?" she exclaimed with a smile on her face. "I've come two hundred and fifty miles to wipe you off that chessboard!"

With that, she wrapped her arms around him. They were warm. He'd forgotten how good hugs felt. He was startled, and his stiffened muscles were slow to relax. Then, on their own accord, his arms slowly moved, hugging her in return.

"My, you're as pretty in real life as you are in your picture," he said quietly, trying to regain his composure. "Please come in and sit down, and I'll put some coffee on." He took a deep breath as she stepped past him and into the humble apartment.

"Let me take your coat. I'll give you a chance to catch your breath before I whip you at chess," he said. Alex felt grateful that she'd come, and there was little doubt it showed on his face.

As he was measuring out the coffee for the electric perk, she walked over and picked up the lamp that he had knocked over and then sat in a chair so that she could watch him fuss over the coffee.

"Sorry for the unannounced visit. I thought of giving you one more play through the post office before trying to meet you. However, my niece was driving up, so I took advantage of the situation and hitched a ride with her." As she spoke, Sylvia lifted her hands to adjust the ivory comb in her hair. "Alex ... in your letters, you seemed like such a nice person. I really wanted to meet you. I hope you don't take offense at my coming ... You don't, do you?"

He paused for a moment before turning to face her. How should he reply? Speak his heart at the risk of coming on too strong? Or play it cool and in control, just like the chess game?

"Silvia, I can't tell you how grateful I am that you

came. I was a little worried that something might have happened to you when I didn't hear from you. I was hesitant to call, not wanting to pry or anything. I'm the one that should apologize, especially for the mess that you see."

With that, they looked at each other in silence, both wanting to absorb the presence of the other and to adjust to another being. The afternoon was fading as they studied one another.

He finally handed her a cup and sat down. "Well, my lady, here is your coffee ... Take it black, I assume? I know that one should never assume anything. It is black, isn't it?"

"Yes, thank you ... You know, you are more than I'd hoped for. I hope you're for real."

"I'll take that as a compliment. Yes, I'm for real. As one might say, 'What you see is what you get!' Remember Flip Wilson? ... Do you feel up to a couple of quick plays before we go somewhere to eat? My cupboards are bare." Standing up and leaning toward Silvia, Alex ran the back of his forefinger down the bridge of her nose with a gentle sweep of his hand and gave her an affectionate smile. "If so, I believe it's your move."

Both retired to the chessboard with coffee in hand.

"It is my move, isn't it? Okay ... white, king's bishop to white queen's knight, five—f1-b5."

EXPECTATIONS

After a while you learn the subtle difference
between holding a hand and chaining a soul,
· ·
And you learn that kisses aren't contracts
and presents aren't promises
· · · · · · · · · · · · · ·
And you learn that love doesn't mean leaning
and company doesn't mean security.

—Author unknown

As she walked down the winding path that early
autumn morning, Gladys could not help thinking
what a fool Alfred was for chasing after Jennifer the
way he did. Gladys's full name was Gladys Amelia
McClusky, and she was almost as masculine as her last
name implied. Her waist was a little thick, hands a little
broad, and shoulders a little too square. Her physical
features seemed to reflect her daily work routine as a
seamstress at Smith & Smith's shirt factory.

It was 1902, and the Gibson girl image was all the
rage, with the pompadour and wasp waist—an aloof

beauty with shadowed eyes that would look down on you from an upturned head. Jennifer had perfected the act and look to a tee. However, Jennifer's act was all a facade, and she had no depth, despite the happenstance coincidence of having the last name Gibson. As far as Gladys knew, all Jennifer had to do all day was primp. She, like Gladys, was eighteen and had just graduated from high school, but unlike Gladys, she didn't have to work. Jennifer did not have to be a slave to a sewing machine. Her father was a local doctor, and Jennifer could afford the expensive clothes and the leisure time, while most of their other classmates could not.

Gladys felt her face flush with anger as she continued walking and thinking about it all. The air was cool and brisk, and her bonnet was tied tight. Her cheeks stung from the wind, and her breath hung in the air in small clouds. She cut through the park every morning on her way to work, heading toward the enslaving sewing machine, where she stayed from seven thirty in the morning to five thirty in the afternoon, every day of the week except Sundays and holidays. She could spend a little more time with Alfred if Jennifer would just go away, say a trip to Europe. Jennifer didn't need Alfred, but Gladys did. She desired him so much. A smile, a touch, or a hello from him would fill her day with joy. Thoughts of Alfred filled her mind from the moment she got up to the moment she closed her eyes in sleep, ever since he had kissed her on that late afternoon. From the moment of that kiss, he was the focal point of her thoughts.

Alfred watched as Gladys approached the fence line that bordered his father's farm and the south end of the park.

I can't let her see me, he thought as he ducked behind an evergreen. *Need to take another route to work! Can't be bumping into her.*

On a previous late afternoon, Alfred had indeed escorted Gladys home from work. He too had been returning from a day's labor as a clerk in the local drugstore. In a lustful moment, he had stolen a kiss from her, and he was now feeling guilty. It was Dr. Gibson's daughter, Jennifer, not Gladys, who was the object of his real affection. Jennifer was the woman whom he could see himself marrying and settling down with. He really shouldn't have given into that impulse to kiss Gladys. What had he been thinking?

The existence of the average man of the early 1900s was as dull as the high collar that he wore. In 1902, he had no such thing as a television or a readily available automobile. For him, there was no golf, and the movie industry was in its infancy. A man's physical acts were his primary source of excitement and pleasure. Given Alfred's options in life, there really wasn't anything to entertain a man in his position. He wasn't the type to go to the theater even if he could afford it. There wasn't much else to do outside of church society, which was not his scene either. So that left the sport of enticing women to a kiss. A stolen kiss was for the thrill of the moment, and that was all. Why did she have to go and read so much into it?

As Gladys and Alfred were about to meet in the park, Jennifer was busy in her bedroom. "Daddy, will you have Alice bake my favorite apple crunch pie for me tomorrow? Everything must be absolutely perfect for this coming Saturday evening!" Jennifer called out as she was going over her wardrobe.

"Of course, dear," her father replied from his bedroom across the hall. "Just leave it to me."

Alice was a maid for the Gibson household who doted on the master and his daughter. The doting was even more so since the death of Mrs. Gibson two years past.

Alfred must do this for me, just this once. If he needs a little persuasion, that can be arranged. A little dessert, a little lace in just the right places, a kiss maybe, and bingo, he's right where I want him, Jennifer thought.

"I've got him. He will be as soft as artist's putty in my hands," she exclaimed. Her gaze was momentarily on the street below, from where her anticipated accomplice would arrive.

Alfred reflected on his approaching date with Jennifer as he tried to remain motionless in his hiding spot behind the evergreen. Jennifer was the heart's desire of the entire male graduating class of 1901 at Eton High. *Jenny has asked me, just me for supper. It was a plea, almost a plea in passion,* he mused. But was the plea real, or was he just trying to convince himself that it was? When reaching for goals, people

will hear what they want to hear. She said she wanted
to be alone with him to discuss some very important
matters. Hopefully those "very important matters"
meant Jennifer was going to be his Gibson girl.

Alfred sneezed just then, and Gladys, startled out
of her reflections, spotted him. "Hello, Alfred!"

Oh no! Now what? Act casual! "Hi, Gladys! I just
got through climbing over that fence." He pointed to the
fence and continued, "I was coming to meet you." He
took a deep breath. "Kiddo, we have to talk!"

"What is it, Alex? Can we meet tonight after work?"

"Gladys, I really care about you and what happens
to you, but I don't want to get involved. Do you
understand?"

Stunned, Gladys just looked at him in disbelief.
"What? Do you mean you don't want to get involved? Is
that what you are trying to say?" With the realization, her
voice rose in pitch. "You kissed me, quite affectionately
I might add. Then you turn around and tell me that you
just want to be friends! Was the kiss just a joke to you?"
She was almost pleading with him now. "How can I
understand? How could anyone understand?"

"It shouldn't have happened ... I am truly sorry."

"You must be ... Get away from me! Stay away from
me!" She started to cry.

"Gladys, please ... you've got to go to work!" Alfred
took her by the shoulders with both hands, trying to
calm her down.

Tears streamed down her cheeks. "Is it Jennifer
then?"

"Yes ... it is. She means a lot to me, you know. Well,
perhaps you don't know."

"You are ... are setting yourself up to get hurt, just like I set myself up for hurt with you." Tears continued to fall down her cheeks as she continued, "You're going to be hurt, but obviously, you'll have to find out for yourself. Don't come crawling back to me when that happens!"

"I am sorry," he said as he let his hands fall from her trembling shoulders. Looking down at his worn leather shoes, he added, "I am truly sorry, and I promise I'll leave you alone from now on."

"Don't do me any favors!" Her face wet with tears and sadness, she turned around and walked toward the factory, toward her enslavement. She called back to him, "Don't ever try to see me again!"

He stood motionless, watching her as she walked away. This hadn't gone as he'd envisioned. He was cold, and the weight of his decision, how he had selfishly used her, was crushing. Had he permanently lost something of immense value, like an heirloom pocket watch dropped in a deep, deep pond? A chill went through him.

It was almost eight in the evening, and the corner gas lamp was lit, shedding its flickering light on the street below, casting a warm glow on all beneath it. The amber moon was full. Someone was burning leaves close by, which left a warm, smoky scent on the night air. Alfred felt his spirits rise as he stood underneath the lamp and gazed up at the big white house that would soon open its doors to him. This was indeed a magical night, full of promise and of the possible fulfillment of his innermost dreams. Thoughts of Gladys fled his mind as he started up the steps.

After the third rap with the brass knocker, the maid opened the door and let him in, leading him to the parlor. "Jennifer will be with you shortly. Please have a seat."

He sat at one end of the overstuffed sofa and stared down at the difference between his worn leather shoes and the highly polished hardwood floor. *All this could be mine someday,* he thought.

"Alfred!"

"Hi, Jennifer! My ... you look pretty."

"Thank you. Are you hungry?" Without waiting for him to reply, she said, "Daddy is out, and we have the place to ourselves. We can talk while we eat. I'm starving."

She led him to the dining room table, where they sat across from one another, and then she called for Alice to bring the entrées in. She reached up and adjusted a pin in her carefully coiffured hair. "Alfred, Mr. Harper is your boss, isn't he?" Jennifer asked while still adjusting the hairpin and looking directly into his eyes.

"Why yes, of course."

"And he places you in charge when he is away on business? Is that correct?"

"Yes. In fact, he said he was going to give me a promotion just after the holidays."

"He must really like you then ... That's wonderful!"

Alfred beamed. He then helped himself to another slice of fresh-baked bread. He planned on making the most of this night.

"Alfred, when we have finished, let's go back to the sofa in the parlor. I've got something to ask you."

He felt a surge of excitement, almost forgetting to swallow his mouthful of food.

The remainder of the dinner passed uneventfully, and after his third piece of cinnamon-crunch apple pie, they retired to the parlor. She sat next to him and took his hand in hers. Her hands were so warm and soft. "Alfred, is Mr. Harper still an honorary regent of Illinois State?"

Puzzled at the continuation of the subject of Mr. Harper, Alfred replied, "Yes, he is, but let's talk about us. It's our future that we have to plan—plan together, that is."

Her petite brow furrowed. "What are you getting at?"

"I'm talking about us ... you and me ... our future together."

After a pause, she said, "Let me see if I have this straight. You think the reason I invited you over tonight was to discuss marriage and all?"

"Why yes. What other reason could you have? I thought we had something going?"

She dropped his hand from hers. "Alfred! Listen to me. I asked you over tonight because I wanted you to do a favor for me. I wanted you to ask Mr. Harper for a recommendation for me to Illinois. You know how hard it is for girls to get into the university. Alfred, I'm not in love with you. I've never thought of you in that light. I just asked you over tonight to ask if you would do me this favor ... Do you understand?"

"Do I understand?" Then he remembered Gladys questioning him with almost the same phrase. Her warning echoed in his mind. He repeated, "Do I understand?"

"Well … do you?"

After a sigh, he said, "You asked me over tonight so that you could get in tight with Mr. Harper, right?" His hands were clasped together and folded in his lap, providing the occasional small self-assurance a man was allowed. He again stared at his well-worn shoes. He didn't see the polished floor this time. Though he was full of dinner, his chest imploded from emptiness.

"Alfred, please, I want you to be my friend and do this one thing for me." She brushed her hand over his knee, speaking in soft tones. "All I'm asking for is your help."

Repeating softly, he said, "You asked me over to get in tight with Mr. Harper?"

"Alfred, I want you to ask Mr. Harper if he will write me a letter of recommendation … I don't want to get in tight with him … okay?"

He looked up at her. The beauty that once had ensnared him was gone. He could see her now for what the hell she was. "I hear you, but I can't do it … Damn it, I won't!"

"There is nothing more to say then … is there?"

"No, Jennifer, there isn't. What a fool I've been."

"Would you like Alice to show you to the door?"

"No, I'll let myself out."

His face was hot against the cool night air. The scent of burning leaves was gone. The streetlamp didn't glow as brightly as before. Even the bright full moon was now hidden behind cloud cover. His body trembled.

"Oh God, what am I going to do?" he asked himself.

"Can't go forward and can't go backward. Gladys will have nothing to do with me now, and Jennifer never wanted me in the first place. What am I going to do?"

Still trembling, he started the long walk home to his father's farm. Alfred could not imagine himself staying on the farm and spending his life as his father had done. Jennifer had been his hope of escape from that future as well as a Gibson girl to hang on his arm. Now there was nothing left.

Looking out through the rain-streaked windowpane, Alfred watched the rivulets of water flowing down the glass. He'd come in early to open the drugstore, but the morning hung heavy. Yesterday he'd been on top of the world, but today he was at the bottom. He turned his gaze toward Mr. Harper's office. There in big chrome letters was W. T. HARPER. Alfred wondered if he'd ever have an office with his name on the door. A marriage to Jennifer would have been his ticket to a more prosperous life, with the subsequent luxuries that he'd never had. Now the hoped-for possibilities were gone forever, if indeed they'd ever existed. He couldn't stay in this little Illinois town of Eton, alone and without change. He'd heard Mr. Harper talk about all the big cities he visited while on business trips. Mr. Harper always shared his experiences with Alfred when he returned. Now, especially in light of what had just happened to him, Alfred wanted to see these places for himself, to experience trains, hotel rooms, and waitresses.

Chicago would be a good place to start, Alfred thought. Of all the cities Mr. Harper talked about, Chicago was the one he discussed and appreciated the most. Noticing that there was still plenty of time to get back and reopen the store, Alfred grabbed his umbrella, locked the front door, and headed for the station house to buy his one-way train ticket to Chicago. He would explain his intentions and plans to Mr. Harper later that afternoon, and he would have to tell his father why staying on the farm wasn't an option, although it might break the old man's heart.

He thought about his actions toward both women as he walked down the store's wooden front steps and headed toward the train station, just a short distance away.

Do I expect too much from others? Do I use people? Perhaps. I used Gladys just like Jennifer tried to use me. Guess I deserved what happened. These weren't the first bridges burned ... When will I learn?

Standing forlorn once inside the station, he heard someone call out, "Hey, buddy! Are you going to buy a ticket, or are you just going to stand there? There are people queuing behind you, you know."

JASON'S GLITCH

Jason sighed and went back to his primary easel. There were other smaller easels scattered about on various tables, but he mainly worked off the big standing floor model, which currently held a canvas in a firm grip. Dressed in his favorite brainstorming smock, with pallet and paintbrush in hand, he stood back and examined his efforts thus far. The painting was shaping up. One could recognize the distinctive '57 Chevrolet lines with the then-popular rear-end fins and unique front end with the two bullet cones worked in the grill and bumper. The tilt and position of the car had to be just right to work with the staged scenic background. Something with the headlights wasn't right; they needed to be a bright yellow. He chose the color lemon yellow from his set of acrylic paints and used a number 8 brush from the 150 series to give the strokes the desired weight and shape.

The telephone rang. Quickly laying the brush and pallet down, he picked the phone up before the answering machine kicked in. "Hello!"

"This is Mr. Withers again. I'm not sure we

discussed the medium or not, but I would prefer you do the ad in acrylic rather than in oil."

Jason gave out a breath of air between pursed lips, thinking he'd dodged the proverbial bullet. "No problem. I usually use acrylic for ads and presentations. Oil-based paint works better for displays in art galleries, art shows, and the like."

"Fine! Then we're on the same page," Mr. Withers responded and hung up.

The phone rang again. This time it was Lisa. She reminded him of their dinner engagement with a possible movie following.

"Yes, I'll pick you up at seven thirty. What time is it now?"

"It's six, so you'd better get hustling!"

"Oh shit! Where did the time go this afternoon?"

"Watch your language! I'm not a street person, remember."

"I'm sorry! I'll wash my mouth out with soap!"

"Oh, you don't have to do that, but at least take a shower," she replied.

They both laughed, and Jason hung up the receiver. He still had a landline phone. Perhaps someday he'd give in and get a cell phone.

"Well, that's enough painting for today, I guess," he said aloud. "Should be able to finish it over the next two days or so with or without interruptions." He attempted to justify to himself that keeping a date with Lisa was a better plan than working.

Jason was indeed behind schedule and had to finish this piece in short order. The ad agency wanted to use it in a beer commercial. The car was to be shown in front of a dance hall of some years back, thus showing to the public the beer's long-standing reputation as the number one choice. If things went well, he would earn a good chunk of change. Jason had earlier suggested adding the hand-painted vehicle to the photo of the dance hall for eye-catching appeal. The major criticism was, why not just simply photograph the subject car? Mr. Wither, however, wanted the just-right colors and positioning and thought a hand-painted version would better achieve the look he wanted for the ad. Besides, Mr. Withers had done business before with Jason on smaller ads and knew Jason could handle this one. Withers Ad Agency was partial to combining what they called real art with photographic art. With straight photographic art, there are always difficulties of dealing with the weather, achieving proper lighting, and finding the just-right auto to work with. Another closing factor in Jason's favor was that time was of the essence, and he was known to be a fast worker.

After showering and dressing, he turned to look at his creation before turning off the apartment's lights. The painting was shaping up well and looked good. He'd captured the image just right. The painting had simply clicked. After stepping out into the lighted hallway and closing his apartment door, Jason noticed a faint yellow light emerging from around the door frame.

"That's odd ... I'm sure I turned all the lights out."

Laughter came from a couple of doors down as people headed out for the evening, rain or no rain. He watched them leave before turning his attention back to his door. The faint light from within remained.

What the hell is this? he thought. Jason tested the

door. It was still locked. He had turned everything off, from the stove to the stereo to the lights. He'd even double-checked to make sure he hadn't left any water running. His phone rang once again inside the apartment.

"Lisa, I'm coming, I'm coming!"

He got out his keys and opened the door. He looked around. The only light now was coming from the hallway. The phone was still ringing. He walked over and picked up the receiver.

"Hello!" There was no answer. He tried again. "Hello!" He tried a third time, a bit louder. "Hello!" Still there was no response.

"What the hell is going on?" Jason said under his breath and slammed down the receiver. He looked around his apartment. All the lights were out except for the hallway light, which crept across his brown-and-beige floor tiles.

The phone rang again. He yanked the receiver off the cradle and almost shouted, "What the heck is it you want?"

It was Lisa this time. "What's going on?"

"Oh ... Lisa, I'm so sorry! There's something weird going on, from light coming from nowhere to the telephone ringing with no one at the other end of the line. I don't know what's going on!"

After a silence, Lisa replied, "Listen, come pick me up, and we'll go back to your place and see if we can figure it out. We can skip the movie, but I am hungry."

"Oh, kiddo! That sounds good. Maybe you will see something that I'm not." Feeling a bit calmer, he hoped she would have an explanation for this.

He stepped out of his apartment and once again locked the door. The light from around the door frame returned, and the phone rang again. Under his breath, he muttered, "Screw you!" and headed for the stairwell, which led to the parking lot. Once outside, Jason looked up into the soft rain, which peppered his face. He took several deep breaths, the cool, fresh air filling his lungs, to calm down a bit. *Just maybe Lisa can figure it all out,* he thought as he climbed into his car.

With Lisa in the car, he drove back into the parking lot. "Are you sure you want to do this? Unless I'm imagining things, it's really weird."

"Come on, Jason; let's go look," Lisa replied as she swept her hand across his cheek.

They climbed the stairs and started down the hall toward his apartment. So far everything appeared normal. However, as they got closer to his apartment, sure enough, the faint yellow glow emanated from around his door.

"Damn, I wasn't imagining it," Jason hissed as he gazed in disbelief.

"Open the door, Jason," Lisa prodded. "Let me take a quick look inside."

He unlocked the door, and she bolted in ahead of him. His phone rang again.

Lisa grabbed the phone and turned to look at him. She shook her head. "Not even heavy breathing." She hung up the receiver.

Together they surveyed the dark apartment.

Catching sight of something, Lisa said, "Jason, close the door!"

Jason did as he was told, and they both then stared at the painting in disbelief. The two headlights that he'd so meticulously painted that afternoon were glowing, emitting light as if they were turned on.

Jason flipped the light switch, and the effect disappeared. Lisa walked over to the light switch and turned it back off. Sure enough, the headlights in the painting lit up. She turned the apartment light back on, and once again everything appeared normal.

"You now have a night-light that apparently is giving off enough energy to trigger the phone ringing. You want to pop some popcorn with it?"

"Very funny! Now what do I do?"

"If I were you and there wasn't enough time to scrap it and start over, I'd finish it as quickly as possible and get it out of here," she said with her hands on her hips, still in a surveillance mood.

"Listen, will you stay here tonight and keep me supplied with conversation and lots of coffee? I'll work through the night. Then we can take it to Withers' office first thing in the morning and let him deal with it. At first, he'll be impressed on my delivering it early—that is, of course, until he notices the slight glitch."

Lisa walked over to the phone and said, "I'll put the coffee on and call out for pizza. You start painting."

Lisa was thinking as she poured the coffee and then asked, "Just where did you get that particular canvas? Was there anything unusual about where you got it?"

Jason responded, "Now that you mention it, there was something out of the ordinary. The attendant at the art supply store at first said they were out of the size I needed. Then he told me of an older canvas up in their attic that's been around ever since he could remember. He had no idea how long it had been up there or why it had never been included along with the main inventory. He said it was already primed to be painted on, though who did the priming and how along ago, he had no idea."

First clue, Lisa thought. "And you bought it anyway?"

Jason responded, "I needed one as soon as possible, and I thought a canvas was a canvas. And it was already primed and stretched on a frame!"

"Well, dear heart, that canvas may have a history."

Jason stared at the canvas as he stroked his brush across it. "If it does, it's too late now."

"Could something have already been painted on it and then covered up with the primer?" Lisa asked.

Jason thought a minute and then laid down the brush and picked up a spatula with a rounded, pointed end. He probed the lower left corner, almost at the edge. Sure enough, a green hue began to appear.

He turned to Lisa. "You're right! There seems to be another painting of some kind underneath the primer. Now what do I do?"

"That's the sixty-four-thousand-dollar question. What options are there?"

"There aren't any! I need to close this deal, or my landlady will ask me to leave."

"Ah, the proverbial starving artist," Lisa replied.

"Not quite as bad as that, but I do want Withers' check deposited in my account, and the sooner the better."

"Well then, patch the corner and finish it. Morning will be here soon. We both need to take a shower and freshen up a bit before traipsing down to Mr. Withers' office."

"I can't thank you enough for staying with me tonight." Jason thought back on his beginning with Lisa. "Our meeting in the university's assembly hall was a red-letter day for me. Who'd ever think that an engineering major and an art major would get together?"

Lisa blushed and said, "It probably happens more than you might think. Give me the keys to your car. I'll run home, freshen up, and be back. You wrap things up here."

They kissed, and she left. He had to admit that he did not know what he would do without her. She was proving to be a lifeline for him, and he hoped that he was for her too, in some small way.

They walked to the office elevator with the finished painting between them.

"What will you say to him?" Lisa asked.

"To start with, I'm not going to say or do anything except present him with his finished piece. I'll deal with the questions later, as they will surely come. Trust me and let me handle this."

"It's your show," she replied.

They walked into Mr. Withers' office and approached the receptionist desk. "Is he in?" Jason asked. "We've come to deliver the painting for the beer ad."

"Yes, go right in. You've been here before." The receptionist was an attractive, middle-aged woman with oversize spectacles and flat-heeled shoes—every inch a true secretary in her white blouse and well-tailored black slacks.

I'll bet there's no screwing around in this office, Jason thought, and not for the first time.

"Good morning, Jason," Mr. Withers said, standing up from behind his desk. "Don't tell me you've finished it already?"

"Yes, sir!" Jason replied, feeling a twinge of excitement.

"Set it up on the table and lean it against the wall."

Lisa helped Jason to gently unwrap the painting and lean it against the wall as directed in a landscape orientation.

Jason held his breath for the response.

"Well done, Jason!" Mr. Withers exclaimed. "Now I can turn my people loose on it."

"Uh, Mr. Withers, could you cut me a check today? You see, Lisa, my lady friend here, and I are going to be married shortly, and as such, we could use the money, if that's all right with you."

Mr. Withers gave a broad grin and replied, "Yes, of course. I'd be only too happy to pay you today!" Mr. Withers called his secretary over the intercom and asked her to cut the check and to give it to them as they were leaving.

"Thank you, sir," Jason responded and turned to leave after shaking Mr. Withers' hand.

Lisa was a little taken aback by Jason's remarks and blushed as Mr. Withers took her hand. All she could think of to do was to give him a demure nod and a smile.

As Jason and Lisa exited the building with check in hand, Lisa looked up at Jason and said, "Huh, what was that? Did we just get engaged?"

He held up his hand and turned to look back at the office building. As the two looked up toward Mr. Withers' office windows, it appeared that something was being repeatedly thrown at the glass.

Not taking the time to answer her question, Jason leaned over, gave her a quick peck on the cheek, and whispered, "Run!"

THE TALE OF CRISPINUS
AND HILARINUS

H aving been granted a day's leave on this the twenty-third day of August in the year 79, Crispinus and Hilarinus, whose station in life was that of slaves to Admiral Vercundus, left their master's naval base at Cape Misenum and traversed the gulf to the opposite shore. The sailing vessel on which they'd purchased passage regularly ferried between Cape Misenum and the western shore of Pompeii, which lay nestled against a gentle slope on the southeast side of the picturesque Mount Vesuvius.

When they disembarked, the still-sleeping city was about three miles distant. Crispinus and his compatriot Hilarinus had to walk the distance, for they could not afford to rent a cart and donkey. Like other mornings of late in Pompeii and its environs, there was not a whisper of a breeze. The day promised to be dry and hot, for not a cloud showed in the sky. A multitude of birds greeted the dawn, and a nearby gamecock gave vent to his familiar cry. Early vendors were arriving with their carts to set up shop, careful to observe the one-way and pedestrian-only streets. The sounds of horses' hooves emanated against stone paving, echoing through the narrow streets.

The two men wore off-white tunics with well-oiled brown leather thong sandals on their feet. They were blessed with strong bodies and stayed in shape, for their master insisted on physical fitness. They were both just shy of their twentieth birthdays but were neither twins nor brothers. Both were pleasant to look upon, with straight noses, square chins, and dark eyes. Crispinus sported a full head of unruly black hair, while Hilarinus' went from brown to red depending on how the sun struck.

Having hiked up from the shore, Crispinus stood at the entrance of Pompeii's western gate—the Marine Gate—which was composed of two arches. The smaller arch was for pedestrians only and the larger for carts and wagons hauling freight and supplies. With broad grins on their faces and with expectations of the coming day's adventure, the two men bolted through the pedestrian arch and found themselves on the western end of the Via dell'Abbondanza, which was the main thoroughfare running east and west across the entire width of Pompeii. As they started their walk down the long avenue, absorbing the sights and sounds of a city awakening, Crispinus gazed again in wonder at the Temple of Venus standing next to the basilica.

"Do you think we should leave an offering at the temple?" Crispinus asked Hilarinus.

"Leave it to you to think of something like that. The answer is no! Our coins will go fast enough as it is without giving them away."

A little farther down, a sign pointed toward a

brothel three blocks up from the Via dell'Abbondanza. Pointing to the sign, Hilarinus asked, "Should we leave an offering there?"

They both broke out in laughter.

They passed the Stabian Baths, crossed the Via di Stabia, and continued along the Via dell'Abbondanza.

The two stopped in front of an enticing *thermopolium* across the street from a fullery, which advertised clean, fresh laundry. Facing the thermopolium, with their backs to the washing and cleaning service, they stood and inhaled the various aromas of hot dishes and breads being prepared, to be served on the highly visible, heated display counters. Behind one of the counters stood Diana, slim of waist with long, dark hair and large, oval eyes. She took notice and gave a friendly wave after wiping her hands on her apron, having recognized them from their last trip. Hilarinus, the more aggressive and taller of the two, returned the wave. Crispinus just stood and nodded as he returned her smile. He usually felt timid and shy around beautiful women, and being in the presence of Diana was no exception.

A shout from across the street made them turn their heads. It sounded like the matron of the laundry service was giving all Hades to someone.

"I wonder where she lives," Crispinus said, returning his attention back to the thermopolium and Diana, who was still visible through the window.

"If you're talking about Diana, don't worry. This time we will find out where she lives before we leave," Hilarinus responded in a matter-of-fact way as he slapped his friend on the shoulder. "If you're talking about the laundry matron, you're on your own, pal."

They both laughed at this.

"We'll stop back when we get hungry enough, and maybe our Diana can spend some time with us after the morning rush," Hilarinus said, somewhat whimsically.

Crispinus sighed. "That sounds good to me!"

They had only enough money between them for two meals each, with sufficient left over to cover their return sail in the evening. Public water fountains were readily available for free drink.

They strolled past the house advertised as belonging to Senator Cornelius Tiburtinus. It was one of the larger homes in Pompeii, opening onto the Via dell'Abbondanza. Driven by curiosity and wanting to make the most of the day, the boys walked off the distance of the front of the house and confirmed that it occupied three-quarters of the insula, or block, facing the street. It also contained a shop, which faced them as well. They had heard their master in conversation saying that the Tiburtinus residence was known to contain many pictorial decorations and furnishings and was the gathering place for the locals who backed his political duumvirate. Indeed, it was said that the senator had a collection of manifestos on scrolls stored in a chest in one of the porticos. These were apparently made available on demand during heated debates, or so the boys' master thought.

Hilarinus and Crispinus both agreed that the sun seemed to be getting unusually hot for so early in the day, and their tunics were getting prematurely stained from sweat. They found a water fountain and availed themselves of the seemingly endless supply, splashing with it as well as taking long drinks.

"When we get our free status, this wouldn't be a bad place to live!" Crispinus remarked between gulps of the cool water cupped in his hands.

"I agree," Hilarinus replied. "I like this place. It's positively beautiful, laid out between Vesuvius and the gulf."

"You're beginning to sound more like me every day," Crispinus said with a smile.

That drew a laugh from Hilarinus as they continued their jovial walk down the street.

The sun waxed hot. The refreshment from the water fountain was short-lived. They regretted forgetting to bring along their sweatbands. Perspiration ran down their faces. They decided to take a short tour of the palaestra, to make use of the public latrine as well as to get out of the sun. The plan was to take a stroll around the amphitheater before making the return hike for something to eat.

Leaving the Via dell'Abbondanza, they turned right onto the Via Nocera. Walking two blocks south on Nocera placed them one block shy of the palaestra, facing its back. The public latrines were on the right of the palaestra, with an outside entrance, so the boys did not have to enter the main structure to relieve themselves. Their goal on this adventure was the amphitheater, which stood along the front side of the palaestra, so after relieving themselves, instead of leaving back through the outside entrance, they decided to walk through the open palaestra grounds. They went around the swimming pool and out through the monumental center gate in the front of the palaestra.

The two entered the nearest archway of the amphitheater and strolled down through some of the long corridors, which were lined with pedestals supporting statues of honored arena combatants.

Always contemplative, Crispinus said while touching one of the stone heads, "You know, if we ever became gladiators and good, maybe our marbled likenesses would someday stand on pedestals like these."

"It could happen," Hilarinus said. "Do you think you would ever want to be a gladiator?"

"A good question. I don't think we will be slaves all our lives. I think Vercundus does want to give us our freedom at some point."

As they turned a corner and faced yet another corridor, three men in clean tunics and about their own age stepped out in front of them. Hilarinus and Crispinus looked at them and then at each other, not knowing quite what to do.

"Who are you, and what are you doing?" the apparent self-appointed leader of the three asked.

"We could ask the same of you!" Hilarinus responded.

The spokesman turned to one of his two companions with a sneer. "Did you hear a challenge in the scoundrel's voice?"

"Listen, we don't want any trouble," Hilarinus said. "My friend and I are on a holiday, and we're exploring the amphitheater. Now if you let us pass, no harm done."

"How heavy is your purse?"

"None of your business!" Hilarinus answered, beginning to redden and lose his temper.

Crispinus stood to Hilarinus' left and scanned the eyes of their three adversaries. Judging by their stance, Crispinus guessed that he and Hilarinus were not going to get out of this situation without a scuffle. As he made a fist, Crispinus braced himself on his right foot so he could put his whole body into a punch.

The ringleader suddenly grabbed Hilarinus by his tunic, whereupon Hilarinus brought his knee up into his opponent's groin. The tough doubled forward with head down, and Hilarinus gave him another quick knee across the bridge of his nose. The other two, one on either side of their leader, made a grab for Hilarinus' arms. Crispinus swung his fist toward the one closest to him, hitting the man in the side of his face and momentarily distracting him from his attempts to restrain Hilarinus. The young man's jawbone cracked under the blow.

Hilarinus wheeled to his left, quickly clasped the remaining hand that held his arm, and continued spinning to his left, dragging the third opponent with him in an arc and thus keeping him off balance. Crispinus swung a punch into the man's stomach as Hilarinus continued to pull him around in a circle. The third attacker stumbled and fell, hitting his nose against the marble floor. Hilarinus grabbed the fallen man's head and smashed it again against the floor.

After an inhale, Hilarinus scanned the three. Tears were coming into the eyes of the one with the dislocated jaw, the ringleader remained in a crouched position holding his groin as blood ran from his nose, and the third one lay curled up on the floor. Determining there was no fight left in them for the moment, Hilarinus turned to Crispinus and said in a hoarse voice, "I think we had better leave now. With our luck, they're probably senators' sons out for some mayhem. Forget about the amphitheater; let's go back to Diana's place to eat and calm our nerves before we sail back."

"I agree," Crispinus said, trying to catch his breath. During the fracas, he had almost forgotten to breathe.

While keeping a watchful eye for the return of their attackers, they retraced their steps along the Via dell'Abbondanza toward the thermopolium where Diana was serving food. With no signs of being followed and cheerful flute music emanating from the Stabian Baths, their spirits began to rise.

Diana was sitting at a table inside the thermopolium, and they guessed she was on her break. As he walked toward her table, Crispinus made one last attempt to brush off any dirt or scuff marks left on his tunic, hoping she wouldn't catch on that they had just been in a fight. However, he could have saved himself the effort, for that was the first thing Hilarinus blurted out.

"By all the gods, you should have seen us in action!"

With a confused smile, Diana asked, "What happened?"

"Three men stopped us at the palaestra. They wanted to pick a fight with us, so we obliged them!"

Crispinus shyly lowered his head as his companion recounted their recent exploit. Diana looked at Crispinus, and he gave her a wan smile. She reached over and reassuringly touched his arm. "Sit down, and

I'll fetch us something from the steam tables. We have an excellent fish stew in a wine sauce, along with fresh-baked bread."

Crispinus looked at Hilarinus. He was about to ask why he had to tell her but then dismissed it and gave his friend a broad grin. They were getting a chance to spend some time with her, and over good food besides.

Almost reading his thoughts, Hilarinus said, "I thought she might be impressed with us. I'm proud of the way we handled ourselves back there!"

Diana brought the steaming dishes over to their table, balancing the three bowls in her arms, and placed them neatly down. The boys politely waited for her to retrieve the round bread loaf and sit before they began to eat.

After tearing off a chunk of bread and dipping her ladle into her soup, Diana said, "Tell me again what the three looked like. Maybe I know of them. There are three well-heeled boys about our age who have been causing trouble in the area. The locals of consequence can't do anything about it, or choose not to, because their fathers are all influential people—two are senators, and one is a magistrate. Nothing can really be done until the *vigiles* catch them in the act."

Diana reached for Crispinus's hand as if to encourage him to talk. Crispinus then took his turn at describing the event and their opponents. After this recital, Hilarinus rolled his eyes in a mocking gesture. Diana laughed demurely.

Hilarinus picked up on her warming to them and asked, "Would you be willing to tell us where you live? We would like to see you again on our next holiday."

Diana blushed but went and retrieved a piece of blank scroll from one of the counters and scribed the Pompeian residence address where they could find her. "I also have family in Rome, but here is where you can find me for the next year or so." She smiled. "Those are my plans anyway."

The three laughed as they parted company.

After it was brought to his attention by his nephew in the early morning of the next day, the twenty-fourth, Vercundus witnessed what looked to be the beginning of an eruption of Vesuvius from his naval base on Cape Misenum, located on the opposite side of the gulf. Vercundus, besides being a naval commander, was also keenly interested in the sciences. He called for a quadrireme—a large ship with four banks of oars— to be immediately readied for a quick departure. His intention was to get a closer look at the situation as well as to rescue as many people as he could if it should prove necessary. He called for his two slaves, Hilarinus and Crispinus.

Crispinus stood on a knoll, rooted to the spot as he looked on at the spectacle. In stunned silence, his thoughts quickly went to Diana. *What's happening to her?*

Hilarinus came running up in an excited state.

"Come! Master is calling for us. We're going to try to rescue a few if we can!"

"We were just there yesterday!" Crispinus cried out.

"Well, things are about to change quickly. Let's go!"

"And Diana?"

"If we can get close enough, we must do what we can. Where she works is not too far from the gate. Now come on!" Hilarinus grabbed Crispinus by the arm, breaking into a run.

As Vercundus' vessel drew close to the Stabian coastline, hot ash, pieces of pumice, and blackened, burned stones of all sizes pelted the ship. On a scroll, Vercundus began hastily recording his observations of the cloud that was forming over Mount Vesuvius.

Later, after interviewing survivors, Pliny the Younger would write the following about the eruption:

> The cloud rose in the sky as if from a huge trunk, expanded, and almost put out branches. It spread like a wide umbrella as it was pushed upwards by the ongoing eruption. Some of the cloud was snow white, while in other parts it was mottled with opaque patches of ash and earth as it spewed forth from the violent explosions.

Shouting, the helmsman turned to the fleet commander. "Sir, we must turn back immediately!"

Vercundus shook his frazzled head in refusal. "Stay the course! We will dock as planned!" His voice could hardly be heard above the cacophony of sounds from the canvas and ropes being stretched to the limit and the frightening rumble of the angry mountain.

Against the bombardment of debris, only a few oarsmen were lost. The others continued to pull at their oars to the rhythm of the drums. Prevailing winds were already keeping anchored ships from leaving the stricken area. Counterbalancing the prevailing winds was hot, heavy air rushing down the mountainside and out to sea, making it very difficult for incoming ships to dock. Crews had to use every seafaring skill they knew to complete the docking maneuver.

A friend of Vercundus, Pomponianus, who resided between Pompeii and the coastline, was in preparation to leave but waiting for more-favorable wind conditions to escape the gently curving shore. Upon reaching Pomponianus' side, Vercundus tried to calm him with an act of bravado by asking for a meal and to be taken to the public baths. Pomponianus first greeted this request with a blank stare and then consented with a shrug of his shoulders.

Middle-aged, balding, and carrying a slight paunch, Senator Cornelius Tiburtinus awoke with a start and tried to wipe the sleep from his eyes. He'd had a bad dream and was trying to orient himself to a new day. Having been a member of the municipal senate for some time, he had angered no few people in his career. Occasionally he would wake in a cold sweat having dreamed of a deceased, vengeful client returning after being cheated out of a considerable sum of money. On the road to Herculaneum, there was already one tombstone outside the city gates that admonished passersby to beware of asking Cornelius's advice and help. Public censure of private or business conduct was read and heard everywhere.

His eyes fell on a basin of water that rested on a stand by the bed. The basin portrayed a semi naked, flying bacchante holding a tray of grapes in her left hand. The sight of the vessel reminded him of the woman he had taken in the late hours of the evening. The scent of her fragrance and sweat still lingered in the bedding as he ran his hand over the coverlets where she had lain. A vision swept across his conscious thought of her slender arms and legs wrapped tightly around him in an embrace.

What was her name? Damn, names don't linger like they used to. She was of no importance anyway. At least she washed afterward, and I'll not have to publicly expose another infant in abandonment. In the harsh Roman society, if an infant wasn't wanted, it was simple left outside to either die or be adopted, and it was the male head of the household who made that decision. Cornelius pondered at the memory of her and dismissed any possible consequences of their sexual union.

As he stood in the couch recess, his temples started to throb. He poured some water from the pitcher and splashed it on his face. He reached for a clean, dry towel from a number his steward had left for his convenience. The time was approaching midmorning, as per the sand clock, which had been presented to him as a gift a few months back. There was suddenly a loud noise, rivaling thunder, that seemed to come from all directions. Tremors rippled through the polished marble floor as he stood motionless in his bare feet. The vibrations became more pronounced. This was unlike any thunderstorm and instinctively felt much more dangerous to Cornelius.

His first thought was that one of the replacement structural support beams of his home had given way. An earthquake a few years back in February of 62 had done much damage to the area. Nero's administration had waived the local property tax so that the city could afford the necessary repairs and reconstruction. Senator Tiburtinus had helped himself to as much of the available funds as he could to beautify and remodel his home.

Rather than look out a window after feeling the tremors, he broke into a run toward the north portico and out into the open peristyle. He stumbled on a loose end of his tunic as he went. Two panicked slaves scrambled to get out of his way. In the courtyard, breathing heavily, Cornelius looked up in astonishment. Not only was the building shuddering, but the heavens had begun to rain hot ash and pieces of rock as the sky grew darker.

"What in Hades is happening?" he cried.

The sky, instead of reflecting daylight with the morning, was blackening as the debris rained.

Having come to pay morning homage, his freedman Titius Primus ran out into the courtyard to join him. They stood transfixed as both tried to comprehend the spectacle.

"Master, what do you make of it? How long will it last?"

"I wish I knew! It seems to be slacking off." *Wishful thinking on my part,* he thought in a rare, fleeting moment of honest appraisal.

Titius shook his head in disbelief at both his patron's opinion and what he was witnessing. The influx of burning debris increased, and both had to retreat under roofing for shelter.

Cornelius turned to his freedman and said, "I want you to stay with me today. I'll need assistance in controlling the slaves and organizing repairs."

Nervous and despondent, Titius considered the fate of his own home and family. He did not know what to say at first. Then in a quiet, assessing voice, wanting to make conversation to assuage his own nervousness, he said, "Sire, like so much in life, I believe the situation is going to get worse before it gets better. Maybe we should hold up on repairs until we know the full extent of what the gods have in mind for us."

"Damn it, I did not ask for your advice or opinion. I want you to do as I say!"

Suddenly, terrifying shrieks of a woman rose from beyond the adjoining wall. "I'm on fire! I'm on fire!"

Cornelius shook his head in contempt. "Who or what is on fire?" he muttered. Ignoring the pitiful cries, he said to Titius, "Gather the hysterical help near the kitchen. We will deal with the problems as they arise. Now go!"

Knowing it would be foolish to ask the senator for permission to leave and check on his own household, Titius began to gather the frantic, nervously chattering slaves. The thought occurred to him to send a runner to speak to his wife and bring her to him. As it was, he couldn't personally do anything about helping them, but at least he would know how they were holding up, if indeed they were. *May the gods watch over us,* he thought.

As the day wore on, twilight advanced, shrouding the vicinity in even greater darkness. Sheets of flame and columns of fire illuminated many parts of the erupting Vesuvius. Their brightness stood out vividly against the deepening shadows. But this was not the first time the giant had awoken and grumbled to those below, so most of the city's populace turned a deaf ear to the seriousness of what was unfolding and tried to return to as normal of a life as they could.

Through the long night, the ground rumbled, and the downpour of debris and ash continued.

Early in the morning on the second day of the eruption, complete chaos reigned in the darkened rooms of the fullery belonging to Stephanus. While the time to wake had passed hours before, outside was as dark and black as night. Upon inspection by candlelight, a good share of the laundry service's clothing—both soiled and sweat-stained clothing that had been taken in during the last few days as well as freshly washed and pressed items—was found to be ruined with burn holes and soot from the falling hot ash. The ash was everywhere, in the press, in the vats, on the floors, and in the impluvium that had been converted into a tank for washing the more delicate items. The tank, which was situated under an opening in the roof to catch soft rainwater, had not been covered in time. The sounds of people coughing echoed out of every home of the city.

"Count the gold and silver coin," Stephanus shouted to his wife of some twenty years. Beads of sweat from the heat and the stress formed on his brow and streaked down his face, and he was covered in fine dust.

"What are we to do? What are we to do?" he repeated to no one as he tried to collect his thoughts and calm down.

His wife finished her count and then handed the bag back to him. "There is a total of one thousand and ninety sesterces."

"That is not enough to cover the damages!"

"Of course, not! That is just yesterday's earnings prior to this mess," she replied as she made a sweeping gesture with her arms.

"What are we to do? What in Hades are we to do?" Stephanus asked hopelessly as he looked for a place to sit down. They were standing in the atrium close to the soiled, dirty soft-water vat. He felt trembling in his legs and was not sure if the vibrations were coming through the mosaic-decorated floor or if he was losing his nerve. Bitter bile filled his throat from a nauseous stomach.

"I told you we should not have bought this place!" his wife said, half scolding—like any good Roman wife. "This was a beautiful home, and we should have left it as it was instead of turning it into a laundry service."

"I know, I know! You wanted to go into the country and retire. You wanted to draw on our savings and live respectably. We did not have to continue working, but I wanted to have one more business success. It appears I was wrong. I'm sorry ... I'm sorry for not taking you into the country as you wished. I'm sorry for not listening."

"What is done is done," his wife said as she put a gentle hand on his shoulder. "Now we have to see what we can do to get out from this."

A loud crash startled them, and the building shuddered, showering them with more dust and plaster. Stephanus looked up and saw his panic mirrored in his wife's eyes. A second crash and a scream brought him quickly to his feet. "Who is that? What was that?" he cried.

Stephanus begun to shake uncontrollably. His questioning cries were answered by more screams. Two of the help came running down the stairs from the ostiary they used as a supply room, located just above the entrance.

Breathlessly, one wheezed, "Where is Messalina? I heard her scream just before—"

Her question was cut off by the rush and noise of lava coming in through the peristyle located in front of the vats. The roof shuddered and collapsed inward as the molten flow poured in from the opening above the atrium.

"No!" Stephanus screamed.

With her arms and hands outstretched, Stephanus's wife ran toward the oncoming tide as if to halt its advance. The liquefied mass engulfed her. Her hair spontaneously flashed into flames as she disappeared.

Stephanus had just enough time to put his arms

protectively around two frightened female employees before they too were buried under the onslaught.

The second day of the eruption found Senator Tiburtinus without sleep. He had been up the preceding night policing and quieting staff while supervising more repairs to his great house to keep up with the ongoing destruction. Debris had continued to rain from the sky since the beginning of the disaster, and the accumulating weight on his roof from the fallout was cracking the support beams.

Not being able to leave his patron, Titius was sick with grief, having already received word from a runner that his home had collapsed. The eldest of his three children was reportedly missing, and his wife would not leave their home without him. Titius could only imagine where his son's body might be wedged, for he both feared and expected the worse.

Senator Tiburtinus and Titius stood, pondering their next move as two more discharges from the mountain erupted above. The last one was the most severe yet, disgorging a thick stream of molten lava that traveled down the mountainside with the speed of the gods' chariots, engulfing all in its path without exception. A beam gave way, and a female slave screamed as she was smothered in pyroclastic material, which now poured in from every opening in the building. Titius had just enough time to turn his head and see the slave's hand disappear into the molten flow as he too was swept up by the hot tide.

Senator Tiburtinus pushed a slave in front of him in a futile effort to block the path of the flow and then jumped up on a stand that moments ago had supported a decorative vase. The hot, acrid air was stifling. The last oil lamp exploded and was carried away by the flow.

"Ye gods, is this it?" Tiburtinus cried out in the darkness.

As if in answer, the superheated flow toppled the stand on which he stood, devouring him in its burning embrace.

A few days after the eruption, Pompeii and the entire Sarnus valley was completely covered in a vast, meters-deep white shroud of dust and pumice.

During the festivities, the chariot races were held at the Circus Maximus, located on the left side of the imperial palace. On the right side of the palace stood the Colosseum, where the gladiators fought. The Circus Maximus was the oldest amphitheater in Rome, originally built some five hundred years prior. During competition, the shouts from the cheering crowds could be heard beyond the city gates. Emperor Domitian freely admitted that though he may well rule all of Rome and its satellite nations, inside the Circus Maximus and Colosseum, the mob ruled.

The Circus Maximus measured about 1,800 feet long

and 600 feet wide. Down the center of the amphitheater ran a long barricade, slightly angled and commonly referred to as the spine. The chariots had to circle it seven times, which amounted to about four miles. In just seven laps the daunting task for the winning charioteer was to capture the inside track as well as the lead position and to hold this place to the finish.

The charioteers ran the elongated circle counterclockwise. In a brace of four horses abreast and attached to the chariot, the near-handed horse commanded the steerage position. It ran alongside the spine as close as possible and was never yoked. The companion horse on the right offside turned the chariot in the direction desired and keyed on the near-handed horse. Both flanking steeds were held with traces and not actually hitched. The two powerful, snorting beasts between the near-hand and right-side positions were yoked to the chariot shaft and did the actual pulling.

The reins were tied around the charioteers' waists, so that they could get more leverage on the turns. The charioteers held the traces in one hand and a whip in the other. They wore heavy leather caps and short tunics that exposed their arms. They all carried a knife in their belts so that, in case of an accident, they could cut themselves free of the reins if there was enough time. In most accidents, there wasn't enough time, and the charioteer would be pulled from the platform of the chariot and dragged at full speed behind the horses. This usually meant death and mutilation for the charioteer. If he survived, he more than likely spent the remainder of his years as a cripple with probable brain damage.

The charioteers raced under their respective colors, which were their team names. In this race, the charioteer Aurelius Mollicus of the Blues had his best horse Volucris on the near-hand side. Volucris was a *Centenarius*, which meant he had won more than a hundred races and wore a special harness. His companion horse on the offside was named Victor. Sandwiched between Volucris and Victor ran a pair of groomed and well-developed steeds showing off plenty of muscle and pulling power.

"There's no way we can lose this one!" Crispinus said as he and Hilarinus both looked down in awe at Mollicus and his chariot team. The participants were being walked to their respective starting positions and, in so doing, paraded in front of the admiring, boisterous host.

Today was the last day of racing, and this race was the eighth in the series of nine posted events. The boys' luck up to this point had not been good, in that they'd captured only one winning bet in the previous seven bouts. The two had spent all their remaining cash on Mollicus. They hoped to quadruple their take with the addition of side bets offered by the bookmaker. They planned on rolling over the potential winnings again on Mollicus for the last race and once again quadrupling their stash with the odds. Crispinus held the ivory markers tightly in his hand for fear of losing them. He didn't trust placing them in a fold of his tunic.

Mollicus flicked Volucris' traces and talked soothingly to the nervous, snorting horses as a groom guided the four-horse hitch into the stall from the rear. Positioned on Mollicus' left and closest to the spine was the Green team, driven by a former slave by the name of Diocles. To Mollicus' right was the Red team, driven by a Greek named Orestes. Farthest out and away from the spine was the White team, driven by a young Nubian called Crescens. The Nubian had the greatest distance to travel to capture the coveted inside position.

The significant advantage of Mollicus' relatively favorable starting position was not lost on Crispinus and his companion. All their favorite had to do was gain a slight lead, cut in front of Diocles, and then hold the lead on the inside track to the end of the seventh lap.

Hilarinus repeated to himself, "Yes, yes, yes!" Turning to Crispinus, he yelled over the din of noise and excitement, "The future is ours!"

The hippomania, or horse madness, had captured all. One woman on the next lower tier was panting heavily. Crispinus thought she was going to faint. The man to his left was biting his forearm. A man called out to a fellow spectator that he would sell himself into slavery to cover his bet if he had to. Another individual was running and jumping down tier to tier to get in closer to the arena floor, pushing people out of the way as he did so.

"Look! There's Diana!" Hilarinus shouted to his companion, pointing.

"Where?" Crispinus cried, turning his head.

"Right over ... over ... Damn, she's gone! I swear I saw her." Hilarinus continued to point toward where he thought he'd seen her.

"Gods! I hope you're right. That would mean she did survive the blast after all," Crispinus muttered. Half out loud he said, "Please let it be so!" He asked Hilarinus, "Do you think she spotted us?"

"Who knows? We'll stay in this spot through to the end of the events and see what happens. I don't think we would have much luck going down to her tier and finding her in this chaos."

The sponsor of the day's racing schedule had climbed the wooden crossmembers and was standing in his elevated box in front of the raucous crowd. He made himself ready to drop the handkerchief—the signal for the crews to throw open the gates, which were located at one end and just outside of the racing circle, for the rush. There were two starts for each contest. The first was the opening of the gates. There was then a race at full gallop to the start line itself. A rope was strung across the start line. If the judge felt the first start was not a fair break, the rope was left taut, and the teams would have to slow down to a stop and return to their respective gates for another try. If the judge thought each driver did get a fair break from the starting gate, then the rope was released and allowed to go slack so that the competing chariots could speed over it—the second start. It behooved the drivers to know the tendency of each of the known judges.

All eyes were upon the sponsor as he stood with his arm outstretched, dangling the white cloth in his closed fist. This was his fleeting moment of glory. Each sponsor in his turn reveled in the power. With his free hand, he wiped the sweat from his perfumed brow. Draped in folds of red cloth, the heralds blew their trumpets, which were also draped in red. The heralds numbered seven, matching the number of laps the chariots would take. There were also seven ornate replicas of dolphins skewered to a horizontal pole in full view of the mob. As each lap was finished, a dolphin would be turned over so the mob could more easily follow the race's developments.

Mollicus watched the outstretched arm holding the handkerchief and tried to keep his excited Blue horse team in check as the chariot surged and bucked beneath him. He briefly blinked his eyes and took in a deep breath. The next thing he knew, the damn handkerchief had begun its fall from the sponsor's grasp. A great shout arose from the mass of humanity. His knees buckled slightly and smacked the wooden front rail as he snapped the traces. The chariot surged forward and swiftly gained speed. The brightly colored rope was still taut across the start line, and in his peripheral vision, he saw his four competitors coming abreast. To his relief, the rope went slack. Now it was no longer a test of nerves but of skill and perseverance. It was down to the business of driving.

Due to the gala festivities, none of the four chariots sported blades extending from their wooden hubs. These blades were used to cut other chariots' spokes and the tendons of competing horses' legs.

Mollicus glanced to his left at Diocles, who was readily showing the whip and smacking it on the rumps of his team. Mollicus knew he wasn't going to beat Diocles to the first turn, for Diocles was fast and, for the moment, held the inside track. There wasn't time to squeeze Diocles into the spine before making the turn. Mollicus would have to take the first turn a little wider than he wanted, which would force Orestes of the Greens and Crescens of the Whites farther out yet. The four were going to hit the first turn abreast, giving Diocles a slight edge, however brief. The disadvantage to Diocles of the Greens was that he would have to make the tightest turn with little room to maneuver.

Mollicus' instincts told him that he would have to smash into Diocles and cause him to crash if he was to beat him. The best time to do it would be when they were making the turn together at the end of the spine. Otherwise, Diocles could pull ahead of Mollicus on the straight stretch, and Mollicus would be forced to chase him throughout the balance of the laps. Mollicus was confident in his thinking that Diocles was his real threat to winning and that the other two would have to chase him regardless of their respective positions.

As they hit the first turn, Mollicus steered his near-hand horse, Volucris, into the side of Diocles' outside horse. He had used this stunt before, and it had always worked. However, this time, his offside horse, Victor, pulled to the right, not following Volucris' lead. Volucris, being pulled in the opposite direction from where he was being guided, stumbled. Mollicus' chariot veered into the Greek Orestes's Red team. Mollicus' right wheel climbed up on the axle of Orestes's left wheel and caught in front of the axle. The quick-witted Nubian, Crescens of the White team, knew there was going to be a crash and swung wide of the locked center chariots, which were in a skid. The mated, skidding chariots slowed just enough to allow Crescens to go around them and make his turn in hot pursuit of Diocles. Not being able to complete the first turn, Mollicus and Orestes together plowed into the barrier at the end of the spine. Mollicus was thrown from his chariot on impact and heard an uproar from the crowd just before he lost consciousness.

Hilarinus and Crispinus sat in stunned silence, their gaze locked on the two shattered chariots amid the fallen horses. This was the day that was supposed to have allowed them a promising future with little financial worries. Now they were financially broke in the heart of the metropolis of Rome with no means of support and no way to find Diana, if indeed that really had been her.

Crispinus felt sick to his stomach. "Now what are we going to do?" he exclaimed half out loud. He stared at the wreckage. Despite the stifling heat from massed bodies in an open-air stadium directly exposed to the afternoon sun, Crispinus broke into a cold sweat. Mollicus was lying at the base of the barricade with his head at a strange angle. *His neck is probably broken,* Crispinus thought. He couldn't take his eyes off the sight, even when a sudden cheer erupted.

The increased uproar, however, turned Hilarinus' attention back to the competition. Somehow Crescens of the Whites had overtaken Diocles and managed to pass him.

Crispinus asked Hilarinus, "How can you watch it, knowing we've just lost everything? We haven't even paid our rent yet for this month." Crispinus had never felt so dejected and empty as he did at this moment. He saw no hope in finding Diana or anything now.

"We might as well watch the spectacle to the finish, since we've already paid for it, and there is one final race. In addition, we should walk over to the Colosseum afterward and take in the gladiator show. Our tickets are good for that also," Hilarinus answered in a reassuring tone to cheer up his companion. "For a while, we are just going to have to live for the moment." Hilarinus then changed his mind. "Actually, if we leave right now, we'll beat the crowd in gaining admission into the Colosseum. There is no sense in our watching this to the end."

"What about Diana?" Crispinus asked in a dejected voice.

"Let her go for now. The harder we try to find her, the more illusory she'll become. Trust me on this. It's the way life is. If it's meant to be and she is still alive, we'll find her. I recall her mentioning that she had relations here in Rome." After a moment of hesitation, he said, "Come on; let's go!"

Blowing out a mouthful of air through compressed lips, Crispinus got up and followed his companion. They both worked their way through the complaining, jostling mob toward the walkway between the tiers.

Once they were outside, the sun beat warm on their backs. They took the cobblestoned pedestrian walkway that led around and along the front of the imperial palace and up to their numbered gate at the Colosseum. Crispinus kept replaying in his mind how they had just lost all their money in one chariot crash. They'd left the family of their late master holding so much promise for the future, and now they had nothing. He turned and looked back and saw others following their lead, laughing and pushing each other as they walked to the Colosseum. All he could feel was despair.

After showing their tickets at the gate, Hilarinus and Crispinus were pointed to the stone stairway that would lead them up to their designated tier number, and from there they found their numbered seats.

After the show was over, Hilarinus and Crispinus stiffly stood up and stretched. They then filed out past the usher, handing back their numbered ivory seat markers, and made for the nearest exit. To their surprise, there was little pushing and shoving among the throng. There were looks of exhaustion and melancholy on the visible faces in the crowd. Turning back to reality was not an easy transition. The games and gladiatorial combats gave the mob a brief respite from the harshness of their lives. And it was no different with Hilarinus and Crispinus.

Heading back toward their abode in the warm evening air, Hilarinus asked, "What do you think the odds are of us getting back into our apartment without being seen by Marcus?"

"He is one tough landlord, I'll admit," Crispinus responded thoughtfully. "For an old man, he doesn't miss anything. Rumor has it that if he can't get his rent by any other means, he has a couple of thugs who will collect it for him."

Hilarinus said, "Well, there you have it. We sneak back, collect our few possessions, and go sign up. I don't fully embrace the idea of becoming a gladiator, but with empty pockets we will have food and shelter. The stairwell is outside and covered, so we shouldn't be seen."

The shadows were deepening as they rounded the corner. The two could make out the outline of their building and their second-story room, which was cantilevered out over the walkway. They noticed movement from two people standing out front, as if on guard. The two individuals were not walking anywhere, nor did it seem they were in conversation. They seemed to be waiting for something or somebody.

"Oh shit!" Crispinus said under his breath as he and Hilarinus quickly flattened themselves up against a wall to avoid being seen. "Could these be our collection boys?"

"It would be a good guess," Hilarinus quietly responded. "I'd take them on with some training, but not now."

"No! Not now to be sure!" After a lengthy pause, Crispinus asked, "Do you have the address for that school?"

Together, Hilarinus and Crispinus took the oath of the Roman gladiator school in front of the lanistae, or trainer. The trainer was a burly fellow with shaggy, uncut black hair, a bull neck, and eyes of dispassionate gray.

"To suffer myself to be whipped with rods, burned with fire, or killed with steel if I disobey!" Crispinus uttered the words of the oath with his right fist clenched and his right forearm held tightly across his chest. He felt sick to his stomach. *What are we getting ourselves into?* he thought. *Have we really come to this? Is this to be our end?* The sun waxed hot, and Crispinus felt himself turning pale and clammy. He wanted to throw up.

Noticing the ashen look on Crispinus's face after taking the oath of allegiance, Hilarinus tried to cheer him up. "Come, my friend; we should eat. They feed well here. If we stay alive, we will be healthy. We'll watch each other's backs."

Belying his stern outward appearance, the trainer, who went by the name of Cornelius Atimetus, said, "Come with me! I'll give you a tour of the grounds." As he said this, he gave Crispinus a quick slap on the shoulder with the flat side of his short wooden sword, which was used for sparring among the inductees. "Cheer up! It's not the end of the world. You may even get to like it. Those that survive actually have been known to retire quite handsomely in their advanced years." He failed to tell them that very few lived to retirement age, at which point they were presented with the wooden sword in ceremony. "We need men like you. Your lives will not be thrown away needlessly. Remember, by the time the Julian Gladiatorial School has finished with your training, it will have invested quite a sum in you."

Ever the one to look at the brighter side of a situation, Hilarinus gave an approving nod as they turned and followed Cornelius's lead. Except for death or the purchase of one's contract, after taking the oath, there was no alternative or escape for the inductee. Since the Spartacus debacle in 72 BC, gladiator schools have kept their trainees and graduates like prisoners.

Cornelius first took Hilarinus and Crispinus to the barracks where the two would live when not in training. Hilarinus and Crispinus were assigned individual rooms, or cells, next to each other that looked out onto the practice field from beneath a roofed passage. The cells were set in a row facing inward toward the open court. Cornelius prodded them to stick their heads in and peek at their new quarters. The sight was not encouraging. The cells were quite small—about ten feet in width and twelve feet in length. Each unit contained a straw-filled mattress upon a stone shelf that served as a bed. There was a niche carved in one wall of each room, where the combatant could keep a statue of whatever god he fancied. No other kind of furniture was made available to the occupant.

As Hilarinus stepped out of his room, ducking his head beneath the door lintel, he proclaimed, "Not as bad as I thought. I half expected to see shackles!"

Ignoring Hilarinus' attempt at humor, Crispinus turned to the trainer and asked, "Are there any bugs or vermin in the mattresses?"

Cornelius answered with a wide grin, which added to Crispinus's dismay. "Bugs will make you ornery. If you are angry, you'll fight better. So think of your little bedfellows as instructors—members of the staff, you might say."

Their walk next took them to the kitchen area and the mess hall, where they would eat in masse with the other gladiators. Cornelius introduced the two to the medico on staff and showed them where they were to go, or be taken, if injured. The doctor seemed sympathetic enough and showed signs of intelligence, which was some encouragement. Next, they went to the arms room, where they would later be fitted out with protective gear and their assigned practice weapons of combat. Actual instruction would be given out on the open field.

Last, Cornelius showed them the prison area for the offenders of school policy. Here they saw leg and branding irons, whips, and shackles, all hanging in neat rows along one wall.

Crispinus quipped, "There are your damn shackles!"

"We just have to behave ourselves; that's all," Hilarinus responded.

Cornelius interjected, "And for really bad cases of

temper and disobedience, let me show you this." He took them around a corner to three very small cells. "In these cells, you cannot stretch nor completely stand up. You must live and sleep in a constant crouching position until we see a change in attitude."

Hilarinus said in a somber tone, "I think you have made your point!"

"If there aren't any more questions, then let's get you fed and outfitted. Though dinner has already been served, the kitchen will feed you on my orders. I want you out on the field by midafternoon. I aim to see where your strengths and weaknesses are, as well as observe your natural reflexes and instincts. Now let's get started on your new careers."

After a hurried meal at the long table in the mess hall, Hilarinus and Crispinus were taken back to the armory and fitted with helmets, padding, and wooden short swords, which were copied from the lethal design and made for practice and mock combats.

Crispinus happened to notice a sand clock as they were marched out onto the open field after being dressed and equipped. It indicated that they were behind in their schedule of activities, for it was past the midafternoon changing of the guard.

The sun is going to be at its hottest, he thought. He was already sweating under his uniform standing there as they waited for Cornelius to join them. He noticed Hilarinus was also sweating. "Is this what Hades is?" Crispinus asked himself, half out loud.

The practice field was inhabited with many gladiators equipped with various pieces of armor and padding. All of them were in pursuit of their individual training. Grunts, groans, yelling, and sometimes screams emanated from any number of the participants and from any point on the field. The noise and din of metal clashing on metal could be heard above everything else.

Finally, Cornelius reappeared with another in tow. "This is Bebrix, and he will be instructing you on the handling of the short sword. He will teach you how to thrust, parry, stab, and hack with the utmost efficiency. By the time he is done with you, you will be as familiar with the implement as with the curves of your most favored whore. Speaking of which, girls will be brought in once a week for your pleasure. I leave you now to the vices of Bebrix." He said the last sentence with a sly grin.

The veteran Bebrix was a stocky, middle-aged man with a scar that ran down the left side of his face, from his temple to the bottom of his jaw, giving him a sinister appearance. He looked as though he was no stranger to death.

Crispinus felt weak in the knees but breathed in deeply and slowly to hold his composure. In silence, the three stood for a moment.

"This is the short sword," Bebrix said with a throaty voice as he held it up to their faces with a broad hand. "It will be forever by your side at all times. You will even sleep with it, and don't ever let me see you drop it."

With the sight of the solitary confinement cell still in their minds, Crispinus and Hilarinus both nodded in full agreement.

Having explained the situation, Bebrix walked them over to two heavily padded wooden pillars embedded vertically into the ground. "Meet your opponents. Against these posts, you will practice the maneuvers of sword handling. You will beat on these wooden soldiers with your swords. When your right arm gets tired, switch to your left. Keep switching and keep hacking for the rest of the afternoon. In so doing, I'll get an idea of what your stamina is. Believe me; it will increase by the time I'm through with you, and you will come to appreciate being able to fight with either arm. Now go to it!"

Crispinus stood for a moment in front of his wooden adversary and then swung with all his might. The impact of the blow sent a spasm of pain up his arm and into his shoulder. He realized that if he were to last for the rest of the day, he would have to tone it down a bit. Sweat flowed down his temples and into his eyes.

Behind him, Bebrix said, "Come on … Come on, people. Pick up the pace! Your opponent would have cleaved you in half by now!"

"Damn Domitian, and damn his lousy chariots!" Crispinus said under his breath as he took another swing with his sword.

"That's right! Get angry—get mean!" Bebrix shouted out. "You're not here to kiss your opponents!"

Hilarinus fared better as he swung his sword, slashing rhythmically, hacking at the wooden post with a degree of visible severity. Within a couple of hours, Bebrix knew which one he would train for the role of a Secutor and which one for the opposing role of a Retiarius, as the school needed replacements for both. The Secutor, or "chaser," was equipped like a Gaul, in that he wore a helmet and breastplate. His

right arm and left leg were also protected by armor. He wielded a sword and protected himself with a shield. The retiarius, or "net man," wore no armor and carried a net and a trident, a three-pronged spear.

Bebrix planned to give them both a week or two on the posts and then start their separate training. It was his conviction that Hilarinus was a natural sword man and that Crispinus could be trained with the net and trident. If Crispinus could not adapt as a retiarius, Bebrix would put him back on the sword, teach him what he could, and let him likely die an early death in the arena. Bebrix had seen a few individuals that looked and acted as if they could play the role but just couldn't for one reason or another and thus suffered a violent death at the hands of an opponent.

Two weeks passed. Bebrix stood watching as the two attacked their individual posts under the hot sun. His first inclination was confirmed. Hilarinus would be schooled as an armored chaser, and Crispinus would be schooled as a net man. Crispinus showed signs of agility and quickness when he made up his mind to do something. Bebrix reflected that if Crispinus could be taught to react without having to think about it first, he might have a chance at survival. Hilarinus, on the other hand, proved to be at ease with a sword. He never lost that whimsical smile. He gave Bebrix the impression that he enjoyed delivering blows. "My work is cut out for me," Bebrix muttered under his breath. "I've had worse!"

Bebrix addressed the two the next day after singling them out. "Today you are going to have live opponents— you will have warm bodies to beat on rather than the

posts. Of course, these warm bodies are going to hit back. This is where your real training starts!"

It had been a long, tumultuous day, and Flamma felt a bit weary after his victory. The outcome had never been in doubt; however, his opponent had taken longer than average to go down. Flamma had finally lost his temper and split the man's skull. He would later have to answer to officials for that. Training gladiators was expensive, and they were not necessarily expected to be killed while putting on a show.

Flamma gathered his strength and went back into the arena to the accompaniment of much cheering. The emperor had once again put up an additional purse if a challenger could be coaxed from the boisterous crowd. Flamma made his customary challenge, holding his short sword high as he slowly turned to address the entire assemblage. The perspiration that continued to run down his face and into his eyes had begun to be annoying. In response to the call, a giant of a man stood up from the fifth tier and began to make his way down to the arena.

Ye gods! was Flamma's first thought. *What a way to end the day.*

The two opponents stood facing each other, both sizing up the other's measure. Finally, the big one said, "I know all about you, but I'll bet you don't know who I am."

Flamma, holding his ground, answered sharply, "Why should I care?" Anger rose within him.

Instinctively he knew this was probably a good thing, for it would channel his focus onto killing as opposed to his adversary's size.

"A few weeks back, you killed my brother in this very same arena. He was drunk and should not have gone up against you. I'm standing in front of you now and answering your challenge to even the score. You know how it goes, 'an eye for an eye.' I'm sure you've heard of it."

The big man was quite calm and relaxed, which spelled real danger to Flamma. Flamma realized that, besides the apparent advantage in height and probable strength, this opponent would not easily be caught off guard and would have to be killed quickly. There would be no playing around with this one.

Just as before, his opponent was handed a net and a trident, and the two proceeded to do a slow, circling dance around each other looking for an opening or a weakness. Shouts of support came down from the excited crowd for both combatants. On the spot, hundreds of private bets were wagered between the onlookers.

Flamma squinted as sweat continued to sting his eyes. Too late, he realized he should have put on a sweatband before donning his helmet. With his sword arm, he quickly tried to wipe his face. In the same instant, he was doubled up from a powerful blow to his midsection that knocked his helmet askew. Then the damnable net was thrown over him. While hacking away with his sword and swinging wide with his shield, Flamma tried to stand up. The slipped helmet briefly exposed the back of his head and neck, as he was still

bent forward. On seeing the opening, his opponent drove the trident down hard into the back of his skull. Flamma saw a flash of white light and then lost consciousness.

Sweating but with a cool demeanor, the big man stood over Flamma's twitching body for a moment and then threw down the trident. Ignoring the boisterous and jeering crowd, not bothering to see whether they were giving him the sparing or death signal, he walked out of the arena through the Gate of Death, not even stopping in front of and saluting the emperor's box. No one attempted to stop him. After a hesitation and a glance at Emperor Domitian, who in his turn gave no sign of recognition one way or the other, the editor of the games gave the sign for the trumpeters to blow their horns, indicating that the entertainment for the day was over.

Diana Secundini now managed one of Rome's hospices for those injured at the games. It was backed financially by a voluntary tax from the game's participants, including gladiators and charioteers alike. Having survived the Vesuvius eruption by leaving Pompeii during the first day of falling debris, Diana had returned to Rome. The family-owned thermopolium in Pompeii had been lost. She'd secured her new position through the efforts of her uncle, who was a senator. Occasionally, the hospice received an additional grant from the senate chamber thanks to this connection.

A breeze came in through an open glass window

as Diana sat at her desk drilling her dutiful, aging, and despondent Greek physician, Phaedimus. The gentle gust ruffled her long black curls, which hung down on both sides of her lightly colored cheeks in the latest Roman fashion. Dressed in a rumpled tunic and well-worn sandals, Phaedimus stood in front of her and answered questions concerning their recent arrival Mollicus, the charioteer. Mollicus had been brought into her establishment just a few weeks ago, after his disastrous crash. His neck was broken, which left him partially paralyzed and in a mental depression. Phaedimus did not hold much hope for Mollicus to be able to lead a decent life for the remainder of his years, let alone ever return to the games. In fact, he didn't hold much hope for anyone, including himself. "We are born to die!" was his favorite quip. The question that continually haunted him was why people were born in the first place. Related to this, Phaedimus remembered the immortal statement of the divine Caesar Augustus, who murmured to his wife, Livia, on his deathbed, "Have I acted out the comedy well?"

"Now we must make room for another, a gladiator called Flamma," Diana said. "He will be delivered to us this afternoon."

"The same Flamma that we hear so much about?" Phaedimus asked.

"There is only one Flamma that I know of," she said, looking up at him as he continued to stand in front of her. "Slaves have already prepared a bed, and I want you to give him a very thorough examination. His renown and popularity demands that we do everything humanly possible for him."

"He'll die in our hands anyway."

Diana snapped her reed stylus in growing frustration. "Damn it, he will receive every chance at life that we can give him, and you will see to it!"

"Okay, okay! I will give him a very thorough examination and do what I can. But don't say I didn't warn you. By the time these people are brought to us, there isn't a whole lot of hope."

"You have your directive; now go! Report back to me what you find and what you've done."

She heard him exclaim under his breath as he headed for the door, "She can be a bitch!" Diana smiled to herself, for she had absolute confidence in his loyalty and skills. Phaedimus had been her family's physician when she was a young girl in her early teens, and she had brought him with her to Rome. Often as not, she had to tell him to take a break or go to his quarters to get some sleep.

In the examination room, Phaedimus looked down upon his recent charge. He sucked in a deep breath between his yellowing, aging teeth as he gently probed the unconscious Flamma, checking for any more sustained injuries. Though Flamma had regained consciousness while being dragged out through the Gate of Death at the Colosseum, he had been quickly dosed with a strong, cathartic drug.

The screaming and roaring of the mob was deafening as Crispinus and Hilarinus stepped onto the arena floor along with the other combatants for the afternoon's festivities. Once again, colored shadows flickered across the whole of the densely packed Colosseum, generated by the wind-blown, multicolored tarp covering the roof of the structure. They entered through the Gate of Life on the west end of the arena floor and marched in formation to the base of the emperor's box. In unison, the gladiators bowed and then stood straight and saluted their emperor. Domitian returned the salute and wished them all a victory.

Crispinus looked at some length at his emperor. *Can he be that stupid, or is he just playing politics? Half of us must lose for the other half to win,* Crispinus thought. "There I go, thinking again," he muttered.

"What did you say?" A burly gladiator hit Crispinus's shoulder with his clenched fist, jarring Crispinus's neck a little. Breaking from his reverie, Crispinus took a quick look around and saw that individuals were pairing off to do combat. The big man standing in front of him was apparently his opponent.

"Are you waiting for an invitation?" the burly man asked derisively while giving a mock bow. Those in the audience seated closer to the two let out peals of laughter, which drew the emperor's attention.

Great, now our emperor probably thinks I'm stupid, Crispinus thought while adjusting his trident and net. *It must look funny, though.*

The two began circling one another, and Crispinus went into a crouching position, focusing on the man facing him. *I must take him down—go for his knees, and stay away from his sword!*

Crispinus felt a blow to his right kidney area and half turned to see who had hit him from behind. At that moment, the burly man thrust his sword into Crispinus's side—just under his net arm. Crispinus's knees buckled as the large man pulled away his sword.

This can't be happening! Crispinus's thoughts screamed as he lost consciousness.

From a quick glance, Hilarinus saw that two had teamed against Crispinus and that Crispinus was falling to his knees. Hilarinus savagely struck out with his sword, knocking his opponent over. As blood pooled from the man's mouth, Hilarinus quickly ran to Crispinus's aid. With great ferocity, he struck down one unprepared assailant from behind with a side swing of his sword, cutting the man almost in half. Hilarinus quickly whirled around toward the other man. The large man attempted to ward off the blow, but Hilarinus hit him across the side of the head, opening a cut down the whole side of the man's face. Hilarinus then followed with a thrust of his sword to the injured man's midriff and left him to die.

Hilarinus kneeled over the unconscious Crispinus. He pulled off the tangled net and saw the wound in Crispinus's side. He hailed two Colosseum staffers who were carrying a litter and ordered them to quickly take the injured Crispinus to the Gate of Death, where doctors waited to accept both the injured and dying.

Hilarinus turned to the emperor's box and saluted. Domitian returned the salute, gave Hilarinus a nod, and motioned for him to follow the litter bearers carrying

Crispinus. The crowd sensed the emperor's approval and cheered Hilarinus. Hilarinus gave a quick bow and took off after his injured companion.

The gladiatorial doctors bent over the unconscious and naked Crispinus, and stripped off his garments to facilitate their labors. They worked at staunching the flow of blood coming from his abdominal wound. When they noticed blood draining from his penis, they looked at each other and shook their heads.

One turned to Hilarinus and said, "We can temporarily staunch the stomach wound as we're doing now, but it appears his kidneys have been damaged. We don't know how severely or the extent of his internal bleeding."

With grave concern on his face, Hilarinus asked, "Is there anyone that can give him further treatment?" Not knowing whether it was true or not but hoping it would bring some promising results, he added, "The emperor has taken a special interest in this man's case."

"There is a doctor here in Rome that has worked wonders—Phaedimus. He is a Greek slave and belongs to a woman who manages one of our hospices. It's been acknowledged that he can work wonders. He is very thorough in his examinations and procedures. Just recently, we sent the famous Flamma to him. I didn't think Flamma stood much of a chance of living, let alone recovering, but at last word, Flamma is still with us."

"Yes, in all haste, let's take my companion there!"

A cart was already hitched to a fast horse and standing by for just such circumstances. The motionless Crispinus was gently though quickly lifted and lowered into the waiting contraption. Hilarinus jumped in just as the driver cracked the whip. If not for Hilarinus' strong arm and firm grip on the sideboard, the jolt would have deposited him on top of Crispinus.

Avoiding the pedestrians-only streets, they careened through the avenues of Rome and around to the back side of an imposing stone structure standing by itself and not walled to adjacent buildings per normal custom. It was late in the afternoon as Hilarinus, covered in sweat and still wearing his gladiator costume, excitedly ran up the steps to what looked to be a receiving dock and banged on the ancient wooden door. He had his doubts but hoped for the best. A dwarfish attendant opened the door and confirmed that this was admissions and that they would receive the injured combatant.

"Please let it not be too late!" Hilarinus muttered under his breath.

The dock was the same height as the floor of the wagon, allowing waiting attendants to quickly step over the wagon's back gate and pick up the litter bearing Crispinus. They proceeded with a well-practiced flurry.

A woman's voice called out with instructions as the litter bearers carried Crispinus in. A moment later, the woman appeared carrying a wax tablet and stylus. Hilarinus, still standing in the vehicle, focused on the tablet and assumed they were going to want some information. Then he looked up into her face, and their eyes met.

"By Zeus, it's ... it's you!" he stammered.

A realization crept onto her face. "Was that your friend Crispinus who was carried in just now?"

Hilarinus nodded. "He was injured this afternoon at the games."

Without another word, Diana whirled around and ran back into the building, dropping her wax tablet as she did so.

For a moment, Hilarinus remained standing in the back of the wagon, staring at the fallen tablet on the cement floor of the receiving dock. Shaking himself from his reverie, he jumped out of the cart, picked up the wax tablet, and ran after her.

After a short run down a corridor, he caught up with Diana in what was obviously an examination room. Crispinus had been gently laid, still unconscious, on a waist-high table. Hilarinus hoped it was the previously administered potion that kept his friend comatose and not the encroachment of death.

Diana stood a little way back from her physician, knowing enough to stay respectfully quiet as Phaedimus did his work as only he could.

Hilarinus walked up beside her and handed over the dropped tablet. With a wan smile, she thanked Hilarinus and then asked him to follow her into an adjoining office where they could sit down and talk while the examination was going on. Though he hesitated at first, Hilarinus let her lead him away, deciding that it was probably best to let the physician do his work. It was becoming obvious that, if the fates allowed, this was going to be the only chance Crispinus had for recovery. Hilarinus reminded himself to later make a sacrifice to the god of healing on his friend's behalf.

What Diana had to tell him, once they'd sat down,

was not a good prognosis. "I'm afraid Crispinus is not going to make it. I have seen several cases pass through here from the games. With observation, one learns which ones will survive and which ones won't. If he succumbs, his grave will be in a well-preserved garden space for fallen combatants, and he will be honored as befitting his rank." In a softer voice, she said, "I know you don't want to hear this, and it deeply saddens me as well."

With a tear-stained face, Hilarinus asked, "Who's going to pay for all this?"

"It won't come out of your purse. Under Domitian's rule, the gaming committee and the school that trained you will cover all cremating and burial expenses." Diana waited for a comment, but none came.

Hilarinus stood up and headed for the door but stopped suddenly and turned around. "After Pompeii was buried, we were hoping you had survived. I thought I saw you in the crowd at a chariot race. Do you attend races?"

"Occasionally. My family has a particular favorite and will bet on him."

"That could have been you then."

"Yes, it could very well have been me." After a moment of reflection, Diana asked, "Will I see you again?"

"Will you watch me fight?"

"No, but I could meet you afterward if my schedule will allow."

"We are given some free time after combat. I would like that very much."

Diana replied, "I know when the games are posted and who, if renowned, is to fight who. If I'm free, I'll come looking for you this time."

"Fair enough!" A wan smile appeared on his sad face as he waved goodbye and walked out the door.

BROTHER MICHAEL
AND KOLA

In a village, just outside the city limits of Nairobi, Kenya, Brother Michael, otherwise known as Erich Braun, stood outside of a dilapidated prison shrouded in heavy foliage. It was six-thirty in the evening and shadows were growing longer. The day remained hot and humid. Per gathered intelligence, it was past the usual last feeding time for the day, and everyone, he thought, should be passive. His hand dripped with sweat from his brow. Wiping it on the back of his pants, he walked up the pitted cement steps to the prison. A uniformed officer who sat by the door and wore three hash marks on the sleeve of his shirt seemed to be in charge.

"Hello! Could I speak to prisoner number seven?"

"You mean Lucky Seven?" the officer asked. He said casually, "I see you're a priest. I've no objections to one priest talking to another. The prisoners have just been fed. He might welcome a visitor now. Granted, not that I care one way or the other."

"Thank you, my son. May I ask why you refer to him as 'Lucky Seven'?"

"Lucky Seven gets unruly occasionally and has to

be taught lessons in behavior. But no bones are broken. That's why we call him that. Besides, seven is a lucky number, right?"

Muscles tensed in Erich's shoulders and arms. Anger's hot breath swept across his face. "Show me to the prisoner if you please!" Erich said between clenched teeth

The officer stood slowly, shrugged, and pulled out a set of keys. "Okay, follow me."

The officer led Erich through the door that separated the small office and the barred cells. A sleepy-looking guard inside immediately stood up when the two entered. Two naked lightbulbs dimly illuminated the hall between the opposite rows of prison cells. Somewhere in the shadows, a toilet flushed. *At least there is running water for somebody,* Erich thought.

"I'm taking this priest to see Lucky Seven," the deputy said. He walked Erich to the cell that held Father Mobutu, and with the sounds of clinking keys and the movement of heavy metal, he opened the cell door. "Hey, get up! You have a guest to see you."

Father Mobutu stood up, shaking as he did so.

In the dim light, Erich could see puffy eyes peering from a much-bruised face. It was clear Father Mobutu had been on the wrong end of some serious beating.

With a practiced movement, Erich moved up behind the officer, pulled out his silenced Daly from beneath his robes, and shoved the cold weapon against the small of the man's back. "Don't make a sound! Don't even flinch!" Erich whispered to the man's sweaty ear.

"What the hell ...?" And then the officer gave out a scream for help.

As the second guard ran down the hall toward them, Erich shoved the deputy's head hard against the bars, quickly turned, and fired at the oncoming second guard. The bullet entered the guard's chest and it exploded as he clutched at his weapon in its holster. He fell to the ground motionless.

Erich leaned over the still form of the deputy he'd knocked unconscious and rifled for the keys. In so doing, he found some plastic handcuffs as well. He cuffed the deputy's hands behind his back and taped his mouth with tape he had hidden under his priestly garments.

Father Mobutu looked bewildered and stammered, "You going to kill me next?"

"No! I'm here to take you out of this mess. Come; we don't have much time. Can you walk?"

"Yes. I'm a bit shaky, but I can walk!"

"Good. Follow me!"

Erich slammed the cell door in a gesture of exuberance. It was then the weight of many eyes watching from behind locked cell doors became tangible. Erich went to the nearest cell. He opened it and gave the inmate the keys and instructions to open the rest of the cells and to all make a run for it. The neighboring inmate gave a welcoming nod of approval and went immediately to his task as Erich and Father Mobutu headed for the office and freedom.

"Bless me, Father, for I have sinned."

"What is your sin, my brother?"

"Murder!" Erich replied in a whisper while kneeling in the small confessional, back in Buenos Aires.

On the other side of the drawn curtain, a stately priest known to Erich from the brotherhood let out a breath of air between pursed lips and asked, "How did this happen?"

"In freeing Father Mobutu." A period of silence followed as Erich mentally relived the event.

"Please go on. Did you feel that this individual had to die?"

"Father, are you judging me? Aren't you supposed to absolve me of my sins?"

Now it was the priest's turn to pause. Then he continued, "I read a Nairobi news article on the Internet about a major jailbreak in which a guard was killed. The authorities attributed the killing and prison break to a political conflict and perhaps confusion." The confessional priest then fell silent, leaving Erich hanging.

"Are you going to absolve me?"

"Yes, of course you are absolved … In the name of the Father, Son, and Holy Ghost, I absolve you of your sins. Go and sin no more." The priest crossed himself as he gave the absolution.

Erich rose from his kneeling position, crossed himself, and quietly walked out. He would leave the definition of *sin* to others. It was his lot to live in two worlds.

The priest returned to his office and called his superior. After listening to the report of Erich's confession, the superior thanked the priest and commended him for a job well done.

"Before you ring off, how is Father Motubu doing?" asked the priest.

"He's doing fine, convalescing at an undisclosed hospital. Erich's confession confirms what we thought. Except for filing your report to Cardinal Riiznor in Rome, your mission is completed. I want to personally thank you for your continued support of our order."

Erich Braun, in the role of Brother Michael, was a member of the Catholic Mercedarians. The Order had been founded in the 1500s and established as a militant arm of the church, created to rescue Christians captured by Islamic infidels. After the African affair, Erich sat resting comfortably in his well-furnished Buenos Aires apartment in the late afternoon. He'd jogged that morning before the heat of the day and finished his paperwork and was now enjoying a cool gin and tonic enriched with a wedge of lime. As a lay brother, Erich could live in the secular world and was not confined to a cloister as a monk was. In the Argentine society, he was also a member of the *Porteños*, or privileged class, as inherited from his German-born father.

Sitting in the comfortable high-back chair with his feet outstretched, sporting soft leather deck shoes, Erich indulged in his iced drink and thought about his run that morning. Running made him feel good physically as well as quieted his troubled spirit. Being a priest who killed was about as dysfunctional as one could get. He gazed up at the calendar on the wall and wondered if 1976 would prove to be a better year for him. The year was still young, so there might be a chance.

He mulled this over as he put down his glass and reached for his favorite deck of cards for another round of Las Vegas–style solitaire—single draws. Playing cards when puzzling over something helped. A good cocktail and a hand at cards beat second-guessing himself or pacing endlessly while contemplating.

The security buzzer rang.

It never fails, he lamented to himself. He got up from his chair and hit the response button. "Yes, can I help you?"

"Mr. Braun, I'm Friar Giuseppe. May I come up? I have an urgent message from Cardinal Riiznor that I'm to give to you in person."

The hidden security camera outside showed a short, balding man dressed in the usual Catholic garb of a priest standing outside Erich's door. Upon studying his visitor through the security camera for a few moments, Erich was confident there was no mischief in progress. The friar was on the heavy side and kept wiping his brow. He looked harmless enough.

Erich called down, "Yes, of course. Come right up!"

Still holding his glass, he let the messenger in. "Sit down. Can I get you something cold to drink? As you can see, I'm imbibing a bit."

"No thank you. I'm sorry if I've inconvenienced you, but Cardinal Riiznor has requested that you return to Rome at the earliest possible moment. I am to accompany you back. He said that you are to be fully packed and that you would understand what that meant. I have a chartered flight waiting for you at the airport. How soon can you be ready?"

Erich let out a deep breath before answering, "Give me a couple of hours to put some things together, and I'll return with you."

"I can help you pack if you need assistance."

"No, thank you. Please sit while I get ready. I've been through this routine before. Judging by the apparent urgency, it must be serious," Erich said.

Leaving Friar Giuseppe seated on the couch, Erich went into his bedroom, pulled out his pieces of luggage, and placed them opened on top of the bedspread. The first thing he went for was his Daly M-5 Commander, which was an automatic made in Israel that fired either a .40 S&W or .45 ACP cartridge. These cartridges were readily available in most foreign markets.

Things will probably get nasty, he mused. In his midsize satchel, he had a concealed compartment that was just big enough to hold the weapon and an extra clip containing hollow-point cartridges. The concealed compartment wouldn't fool customs if he was taking a commercial flight, but it might fool the average bloke who got it into his or her head to rummage through his belongings in a brief absence. Before snapping the last piece of luggage shut, Erich paused for a moment and then threw in a couple of decks of cards. *In this game, one never knows.*

When Erich set the packed valises by the door, the middle-aged friar stood up to leave.

"Just a moment," Erich said. "I have to make a call to my neighbor and ask him to look after the place while I'm gone. He's done this for me before."

"Fine. I'll carry your luggage down to the rental car while you finish up."

It was late in the afternoon when the Vatican jet lifted off the runway with both Brother Michael and Friar Giuseppe on board. Erich sat across from the good friar. He gazed out through the glass, watching puffs of cumulus clouds as the plane banked and then climbed to a cruising altitude. It would be a few hours before the jet touched down in Rome.

I hope he doesn't snore, Erich thought, giving a silent chuckle. *Now to get serious. Aw shit, I'll get a drink first after the clearance is given to unbuckle, and then I'll get serious. I wonder what's up. Probably I'll be forced to take somebody down and then do the required penance or at least go through the motions of it, anyway.*

Sometimes Erich did feel truly penitent, but other times the target really deserved it and the world was better off. For him personally to get to heaven, Erich believed he would need a lot of intercedences. His soul was in the Vatican's hands, and he would do what he had to do and let others answer for it. He wondered how much Cardinal Riiznor told His Excellency the pope. If the pope asked for physical intervention, it came down through the short chain of command. Sometimes Erich wondered how much information went up from Riiznor to the pope. Probably best he didn't know, but Erich privately questioned it occasionally.

Erich reached for the small valise that held the

cards. He pulled the jokers out of a selected deck and then shuffled. The first seven card placements weren't a bad hand—three low cards, three face cards, and the ace of spades.

"Interesting!" he muttered under his breath. He then proceeded to lose himself in his game, however brief it might prove to be.

Under a heavily clouded, darkening sky, a cold north wind blew in from the Barents Sea, following the path of the Kola River, and whipped around the ashen-gray buildings of Murmansk, Russia. In a third-story, sparsely furnished, one-room apartment, a lightbulb hung lazily from the buff-painted plaster ceiling. A scuffed wooden desk and chair stood by a wrought iron bed covered with a well-used bedspread. A small porcelain sink stood in a corner. A community bathroom facility was located down the adjoining hall outside of the apartment. It was here that five fugitives found themselves after fleeing the Kola well.

Standing, former project manager Surgey Rostikov, in his thick Russian accent, said, "I apologize for the accommodations, but we couldn't go to just any public place, as they forward their listings to the authorities every night. The people who own this building have been vacationing in the Crimea, and the building manager is a distant relative of mine. If neighbors talk or ask questions, he'll … take care of things."

On the bed sat Dr. Jennifer Perez along with her lab assistant, Neal Cummings. Speaking up for himself and the group, Neal replied, "Don't worry about the accommodations. Having just got here, we appreciate you finding a place on such a short notice."

Former drilling foreman Stefan Rantanen, who had commandeered the single desk chair, simply shrugged his shoulders. He had no problem with Neal attempting to be the spokesperson. He wasn't sure he was even going to stay with these people. Being half Finnish and half Russian and fluent in Russian, Finnish as well as English, he could quickly lose himself among the citizenry if push came to shove.

Stefan patted the vial of seepage from the well in his leather jacket. If he decided to split company and go his own way, at the very least he could use it on himself should the need arise. Stefan leaned back in his chair and pondered, watching the others.

Sitting on his haunches with his back against the wall, Father Dominick, who was an Italian Catholic priest, stood up and cleared his throat. "I have a suggestion. It's a long shot."

"Let us be the judges," Stefan mused out loud as he turned his attention to the priest.

"Well, we have to get out of Russia, and we'll need a temporary haven once we do. We are just a few miles from the Finnish boarder. In Finland, there is a monastery at Valamo that'll offer us sanctuary. Once there, a Cardinal Riiznor has promised to send someone to meet us and to fly us out of Finland to Rome. The Catholic Church has taken a keen interest in the rumored healing properties of the seepage captured from the well. That is why I was at the site in the first place, though admittedly in an undercover role, as you found me."

Ignoring Dr. Jennifer Perez's cautioning hand on his arm, Neal testily said, "You had this plan already mapped out! Why didn't you tell us this before? Did you know things were going to end badly and we'd end up being pursued by god knows who all?"

Father Dominick answered in a cool, monotone voice, "I was following Cardinal Riiznor's orders, and he felt, as did I, that it would not hurt to leave an opening for me and anyone else with me in case things turned ugly, as they indeed did. Not saying anything to you until now was a matter of prudence. Quite frankly, I had to know who was in and who was out since my life is also on the line."

Stefan gave the priest a slight smile and nodded in approval.

Now Jennifer intervened and turned to Stefan. "The material did show some promise of doing what everyone seems to hope for. And for whatever advantages it might offer, the Russian Mafia apparently wants to control it. If there is money to be made, they want to be the ones making it."

Stefan said, "If the church at Rome wishes to fly us out of our predicament, I think it would be wise to accept the offer and to turn the vial over as payment for this service. Besides, there might be some well-earned compensation for the hell we went through. It sounds reasonable to me."

Jennifer gave Stefan a quizzical look but said nothing.

Father Dominick looked around at the heads nodding in agreement and pulled out his phone.

A loose windowpane rattled from the wind, and the lone lightbulb flickered. Fatigue showed on everyone's faces. The men were unshaven, and Jennifer's hair was a bit matted. There was a knock, and Surgey ambled over to the door and opened it slowly to reveal a short, squat individual whom he introduced as the building manager.

After introductions, the newcomer turned to Surgey. "There is a man's body lying downstairs in the hall by the main door. It looks like he was beaten up. Anyhow, I called the authorities, and the body will be removed in the morning. It must be a busy night for the *politsiya*. I tell you this so you will not be alarmed if you leave the building tonight and see him lying there. If you are here by morning, I ask that you stay in this room till the situation downstairs, shall we say, is cleared."

Surgey warmly thanked him for the information and for his continued cooperation and then escorted him to the door while stuffing a few extra rubles into his extended hand. Before closing the door, Surgey called after his cousin and asked, "Do you know where else would be available to us for a few hours tonight?"

The fat little man stopped in his tracks and thought for a moment. "Wait a minute, of course! My brother is the night guard at the carnival on the south end of the city. He works alone but has a transmitting radio receiver. He reports into city hall every two hours throughout the night after making his rounds. He could put you up temporarily in the tent he uses for an office. If a police cruiser were to stop by and ask questions, he could introduce you as family in town for a visit. You would have to be out by seven in the morning so as not to put him at risk, as his shift ends at eight."

"When does he go on duty?" Surgey asked.

"The carnival closes in the spring months around seven in the evening, so it would be reasonably safe to pay him a visit around eight o'clock."

Leaving the apartment door open, Surgey walked down the hall to where his cousin stood and gave him a Russian embrace. Surgey said quietly, "Call your brother and make the arrangements for my party. Tell him it's just for tonight. We will leave in the morning before the place opens. Also tell him that I will compensate him for his troubles." Surgey slipped a few more bills into the man's jacket pocket and went back to tell the others.

Surgey returned to the apartment and told the group what he had planned, ending by saying, "You may have glimpsed the grounds upon our entering Murmansk. I tell you in case we get separated for one reason or another."

Father Dominick was the first to reply. "Heaven forbid it!" he said as he crossed himself. He then said, "We'll have to leave tonight. We can't risk getting caught in a room-to-room search by authorities because of a dead body. We must also assume the Russian mob has its tentacles in the Murmansk police force." Turning to Surgey and putting a hand on his shoulder, Father Dominick continued, "Thank you for a little respite. You do understand that we must leave this apartment this evening and probably as soon as possible. Overall it's a good plan. It's best we travel to the Finnish border in daylight since more people will be about and we won't stand out as much. I can have the local priest pick us up at the carnival grounds in the morning and take us to the border." Turning to the rest, he asked, "Are we all in agreement?"

"Why can't the priest pick us up tonight?" asked Neal.

Father Dominick was quick to reply. "We can't put him or his sanctuary in jeopardy by moving about with him any more than we have to. We are taking a chance in leaving here tonight and driving our own car over to the carnival grounds, but that is the risk we'll have to take."

Father Dominick gave an affirmative thumbs-up and told Surgey to go down to the front office and confirm arrangements since everyone was on board with the plan. At least, no one made any outright objections.

Stefan gave Jennifer a slight smile, and to Stefan's surprise, she returned it and nodded, even as tired as she was. Neal caught the two looking at each other. He fidgeted a bit but didn't comment.

Surgey returned with confirmation of their fairground accommodations for the night. The five filed out of the apartment and headed for the stairwell since there were no elevators in the building, nor would they trust any had there been. While clambering down the stairs, Stefan had the crazy thought that life is always lived looking forward but only understood backwards. *Someday this scramble might make sense,* he thought.

All five looked at the dead body as they exited into the cold evening air.

Cardinal Riiznor's office, located in the Pontifical Academy of Sciences building, was almost in the center of Vatican City. His office had direct cable links to the twin-towered, steel-girded Marconi transmitting station on the western end of the city. Both encrypted and unencrypted messages as well as regular radio and television broadcasts were transmitted all over the world from here.

It was early in the morning, so Riiznor's secretary wasn't in the outer office. As such, Erich walked right through and rapped on Riiznor's door.

"Come in."

Opening the door, Erich was surprised to see Cardinal Riiznor dressed not in his full church regalia but in a pullover underneath a black knit shirt, black trousers, and no cap. The bareheaded Cardinal Riiznor stood up from behind his desk and held out his ringed hand to Erich.

"Sit down, Erich. I'll give you a quick brief. First, have you ever heard of the Kola well, or the Kola superdeep borehole?"

"No, can't say that I have. I know there's a Kola Peninsula in Russia off the Barents Sea."

"Correct! On that site, there has been some drilling down to about 12,262 meters, or 40,230 feet. The Russians had to stop drilling because the operating temperature down there at three hundred degrees Celsius was destroying the drill bits."

"Interesting, but why am I here?"

"I'm coming to that. There is seepage creeping up the shaft that may or may not have some special characteristics. It is rumored that some local farmers got a hold of a bit of this material and healed some of their aches and pains with it. In the right hands, it might have some significant healing potential and could even combat serious illnesses. Also, it could be an extremely potent and virulent mutagenic pathogen. This aspect has drawn military interest to the substance. It is believed that it is made up of dead plankton and other assorted organisms. The pope thinks we should look at it in one of our labs. This substance could be a sample of what learned professionals are starting to call *black ooze*. It is in the form of a mineral oil, possibly containing amounts of m-state gold and iridium. The substance also shows the ability to self-organize in different ways and has been reported to carry a highly intelligent consciousness. Anyway, some of our people have acquired a sample of the seepage substance and have had to flee to Finland with it to preserve the sample and themselves."

Sensing the conversation was coming around to his role in the situation, Erich asked, "So who is chasing them and why?"

"The Russian Mafia. When the word got out that people in high places were taking an interest in the substance, the Mafia became interested too. Flat out, their interests are money and control."

"I know where this is going," Erich replied. "I'm to

go to Finland, gather them up before the Russians find them, and whisk them safely back here."

"Here's the dossier," Cardinal Riiznor said as he handed Erich a thick sealed envelope. "Absorb it and study the five enclosed photographs on your flight. One is of a priest named Father Dominick, who represents our interests. Next there is Dr. Jennifer Perez and her assistant, Neal Cummings, representing the scientists involved. Another is Surgey Rostikov, a Russian friendly and one of the three head engineers. Lastly there is Stefan Rantanen, principal foreman of the drilling operation. He was recruited by Rostikov. He's half Finish and half Russian and is former military. He's the one carrying and guarding the sample. You are to meet up with them at the Valamo Monastery in Finland. Right now, the monastery is acting as a temporary safe house. The situation won't last for long. I want all five safely back here for debriefing and rest. They have been through a lot. Good luck, and may God go with you!"

"I'll take a quick shower and shave, get something to eat, and get ready to fly out. I can get some rest on the plane."

"Correction: you have to get back on board now!"

Erich slowly blew out some air between pursed lips and gave a nod. "Okay, time is short. I got it."

"If you have any questions, you can call me directly once you're on the plane. The phone system is safe and secure. I'll be staying close to my office all the while you are gone. I may actually sleep here."

"I was hoping for at least a shower and breakfast."

"You don't have time for a shower. As for breakfast,

Friar Giuseppe is making arrangements to have it brought on board for both of you."

"He could have told me," Erich quipped.

"Don't be too hard on him. The good friar didn't know about leaving so soon either. He was informed at the airfield."

"Is the situation out of control?" Erich asked.

"Not quite, but time is short, and things could unravel quickly, so use your judgment. Do you understand?"

"I am completely packed," Erich responded, gazing directly at Cardinal Riiznor with a knowing look. Erich's adrenaline began to flow. "What about Friar Giuseppe?"

"He's to accompany you on this mission, and you're to use him only as much as you have to. Share with him only as much as you feel he needs to know—nothing more. I'm turning this office into something that might resemble a command center." After a pause, he added, "Oh, I almost forgot. You and Friar Giuseppe will be flying in a private charter jet. You will not be flying into battle, so to speak, with the normal Vatican colors."

Erich had been involved in too many situations before to be surprised by the plane switch. *This might be interesting,* he thought as he turned and headed for the door with the brief under his arm.

Friar Giuseppe was waiting for Erich in an electric car at the heliport pad that the Vatican used for shuttling VIP visitors between Vatican City and Rome's airport.

"Come; I'll drive us to our plane. As you probably

already know, this all came as a surprise to me also. But we must do what we must do."

"Aren't you profound for so early in the morning," Erich responded somewhat sarcastically, but then he patted the friar on the shoulder and gave him a nod of approval.

They pulled up along the left side of the parked Learjet. It was painted white with a red stripe that ran the length of the fuselage. Its only other markings were the black call numbers painted on the tail. The engine pods were back by the tail, making for a long, sleek body.

The wind began to gust, cooling the air. Thunder rolled across the heavily clouded, darkening sky as if in warning. Looking up toward the heavens, Erich said, "I don't think a little rain will stop this baby."

As Erich was studying the sky, a door, located behind the pilot's window, opened and lowered to reveal steps. The set of folding steps lowered and unfolded, extending almost down to the tarmac. A figure appeared in the open doorway and greeted them. "Welcome! Feel free to climb on board. We're ready when you are. I am your captain. My copilot is conferring with the control tower as I speak."

Friar Giuseppe helped Erich with his luggage. Erich took an immediate liking to the brisk, businesslike attitude of the pilot. Erich was always suspicious if a person became too wordy over simple actions. It might mean that he or she was attempting to cover up something. Erich also appreciated that the pilot was well dressed in pressed black slacks, white shirt, and tie. Stepping up into the cabin, Erich shook hands with the pilot after introductions were made. He was then led to the pilot compartment and introduced to the copilot, who was busy going over the preflight checklist. The copilot, who was sporting a headset with a small, protruding microphone, was dressed like the pilot and was quite cordial even though interrupted from his task. Both men were middle-aged, clean-shaven, and well-groomed with short haircuts—every appearance of professionalism.

Leaving the pilots to do their work, Erich went to his seat. A quick scan of the interior of the jet revealed a very comfortable business setting consisting of light-beige leather, high-back seating for eight, an easily accessible flight phone recessed into the cabin wall, and a refreshment center toward the front just before the pilot's compartment. The short-pile carpet was a light brown, and in the back, there was a full lavatory closed off in a rich mahogany wood finish.

Erich and Friar Giuseppe settled into their seats and buckled in for takeoff. Erich was positioned close to the phone in one of the three seats that had a foldaway desk readily available.

"I assume that there is a breakfast of some sorts on board. I'm starved!"

Friar Giuseppe laughed. "Yes, we are quite well stocked for not having a galley. There's a good supply of refrigerated taco mix and shells, ham sandwiches, fruit, an assortment of chips and salted nuts, and bottled water, flavored and unflavored. And, of course, there's beer, gin, and tonic water."

Erich smiled. "No booze for me. I'll wait until I get these people back, whomever they are. Help yourself, but watch it! If I need you, I want you sober ... understand?"

"Don't worry about me. My preference is beer, and I know my limit."

The two jet engines began to whine in a higher pitch, and the sleek plane started to roll forward toward its cleared path.

Over the noise of the engine pods, Friar Giuseppe shouted, "It's a Learjet, a Bombardier if I understood them right!"

Erich nodded and rested his head against the seat, anticipating the surge of power that would propel them. He looked out the window. Just a few droplets of water appeared on the plexiglass and almost immediately streaked off.

Over the intercom, the pilot announced, "There's a storm front moving in. Make sure you're strapped in, for there may be some turbulence until we climb above it. We'll be in the air for about five hours. Helsinki is reporting fair weather, so there should be no problems. Other than that, enjoy the flight, and thank you for choosing our firm."

No problems. If they only knew, Erich thought with a quiet laugh. He glanced at Friar Giuseppe, who was bracing himself for the takeoff. The jet surged, pushing Erich back against his seat. He closed his eyes. His thoughts turned back to that day in the chapel one Sunday morning in Buenos Aires when he had just turned seventeen.

On this Sunday, a visiting priest had been quite active in delivering a sermon on certain evils of the world, preaching in a loud, high-pitched voice and gesticulating with his hands and arms. The young minister of God had put his whole self into his sermon, so much so that the veins in his neck started to noticeably stand out against his highly starched white collar.

"... You must not look on the world and its material wealth. You must look above for the things that really count in this life. With that faith, you can be under the spiritual healing power of the Almighty. Listen to me, brethren—I'm preaching my heart out here!" His Spanish tongue carried a slight American accent, perhaps western American.

Erich wondered what would happen if indeed one of the visiting minister's veins really did pop. He pictured the young priest wildly preaching with blood running out of his mouth and neck. That would have kept the congregation awake and riveted to their seats.

While the frocked priest was carrying on, Erich glanced out a partially opened church window close to where he was sitting. He saw a young woman swinging on a swing. Erich guessed she was just a little older than he was. She was slight of body with fair skin and long coal-black hair falling over her shoulders. She wore a bright-red tank top with a short blue denim skirt and no shoes. As she swung, her short skirt inched up her bare thighs, higher and higher with each swing of her body, in rhythm with the minister's voice getting louder and louder. The situation promised quite a crescendo. He sat, spellbound by the incongruity of the whole scenario. Would the veins pop in the visiting minister's neck, or would the young woman's skirt reach, or even go up over, her panty line, if indeed she wore any? It was a race between the two, but to what imaginary finish he wasn't quite sure. Would the minister end up lying on his back with blood spurting from a bulging neck with his arms still thrashing, or would the young woman end up completely naked while gently swinging? Or maybe both?

Suddenly, choir music filled the air, drawing his attention away from the window scene back to the priest, who apparently had finished his sermon and now was returning to his seat. Erich glanced back to the open window and saw that the swing and its occupant were slowing down into a drift. Her skirt stopped midway in its climb. The young woman turned her head as if being called by someone.

The sun piercing through the window and a roll of the plane woke Erich. He looked at his watch. They were an hour into the flight. He had to review the brief, make some plans, and get something to eat, and he only had four remaining hours at the most to do it before they landed in Helsinki. A glance over at his companion showed Friar Giuseppe fast asleep.

"Damn! Let's eat first and then get cracking," he muttered quietly.

After eating, Erich cleared the table except for a bottle of water and laid the brief open in front of him. He first examined the picture of Dr. Jennifer Perez and the dossier of her life and accomplishments. Then he looked at the picture and data for the Kola well's principal engineer, Surgey Rostikov. He reviewed the remaining pictures and info for the group and then moved on to the picture and dossier for the outcast who was reportedly in chase of the group, Casimir Karpov—hired gun for the Russian mobster Kostya Yermakov. After laying out all six photos along with their corresponding dossiers, he had a pretty good appreciation of the size of the challenge that awaited him.

I've heard about this Kostya Yermakov. So that's who I'm up against. If he's hired this Karpov, Karpov must be good at his work. Yermakov wouldn't settle for just anybody to do this job. I can give this man no quarter, which means eating and sleeping with the Daly and keeping Friar Giuseppe in my rear. Good intelligence on Riiznor's part.

The hired gun probably works alone and may or may not be in disguise. Judging from his looks, with his soft gray eyes, close-cropped beard, and short, unruly hair, he's probably quite a charmer when he wants to be—all in all a very dangerous individual. This Casimir Karpov could walk right up to them, and they wouldn't have a clue—that is, until the muzzle flashed.

If I find them alive, absolutely no strangers get next to them in whatever capacity. I'll have to herd them like sheep with a wolf on my tail. If it is decided that Karpov needs assistance and others are sent with him, it might create a little confusion for Karpov to sort out. That might buy me some time at a crucial moment.

Erich took a sip of his bottled water and leaned back in the seat. *So much for leaving Giuseppe in Helsinki. He's going to have to come with me all the way into*

Joensuu. We'll have to get everything the plane will need for the return trip in Helsinki. No one comes near the jet in Joensuu—no mechanics, no caterers, no one. That's where Giuseppe comes in. He'll have to hold his ground while I'm at the monastery.

"Attention: we'll be landing in Helsinki in approximately forty-five minutes," a voice called out over the speaker system, breaking Erich from his thoughts.

"Okay, time to put on the priestly garb," Erich said quietly to himself. Still sleeping, Friar Giuseppe had awakened only long enough to eat and go to the washroom.

Let him rest while he can, Erich thought. *He can grab a shower in a man's facility at the Helsinki Airport before we continue to Joensuu.*

Erich walked past the sleeping friar to the pilot's compartment door and knocked. The whine of the jet engines was enough to drown out all the lesser noises, and Erich wondered if the pilots would hear him.

"Come in!" came a reply from inside.

When Erich opened the compartment door, the pilot asked, "Well, Father, what can we do for you?"

"Here's what I'd like you to do. I don't want anyone to come near this plane in Joensuu, not even to service it. Therefore, I want all refueling and resupplying of foodstuffs, such as there is, done in the Helsinki-Vantaa Airport. I want you two to remain on board and alert for any infraction of my instructions. Friar Giuseppe will remain on board with you in Joensuu, and he'll be in constant communication with me. I'd like for us to be parked in Helsinki just long enough for the plane to be serviced and for Friar Giuseppe to take a quick shower. Then we'll take off. Do you have any problem with that?"

Both pilots shook their heads.

"Fine. If there are any additional charges for what I ask you to do, don't hesitate to bill us. The success of this flight is very important."

Both pilots gave him a thumbs-up in response. Erich gave them an affirming nod of approval and returned to the sleeping friar.

"Wake up, Friar! We're almost there," Erich said while giving his companion's shoulder a shake.

"Okay, okay, I'm awake!"

Erich relayed the plan he'd given the pilots. "Besides a quick shower, from here on, I want you to stay on board with the pilots. Nobody is to come near this plane once in Joensuu. Stay close to the in-flight phone and alert me to anything that doesn't look right to you. I'll be the judge as to what to do next. I will go by car to the monastery to collect my charges."

Erich handed Friar Giuseppe a few selected pages from Cardinal Riiznor's brief. "Read this as soon as you can and memorize the photo of Casimir Karpov. If you even get a hint of this individual's presence, I want you to tell me immediately."

A sharp announcement came over the speaker system. "Buckle up, as we're approaching the landing pattern for Helsinki-Vantaa Airport."

The aircraft banked slightly toward the left, and Erich grabbed for his seat. The jet glided down in a casual descent and touched the tarmac without a single bounce. *Professionals all the way,* Erich thought.

The flight phone rang, and Erich picked up the receiver after unbuckling.

"How was your flight?" Not waiting for a reply, Cardinal Riiznor continued, "You'll have a secure place to park the plane in Joensuu. A chauffeured white Mercedes will be waiting to take you to Valamo and back. From now on, you are Brother Michael and stay as Brother Michael until we confer back here in my office. Your charges are to know you only as such. Your chauffeur will be in uniform and is one of my plants. The password is 'cherry red,' and he'll reply, 'Blossoms are in bloom.' He'll be packing in case things really get messy. The car is equipped with a secure phone. I'll be in touch throughout this whole episode. Do you have any questions?"

"No. I suspect that Karpov will be coming at us alone, and I'm taking precautions. I know things can always change, but my instincts tell me he'll be alone and not with distracting team members. I've briefed Friar Giuseppe on Karpov, and he, along with the two pilots, will stay on board for the duration of the mission from when we leave Helsinki. So, as a good cardinal ought to do, pray for your subjects."

Riiznor laughed at this and wished Brother Michael good luck.

In Helsinki, Erich, now Brother Michael, stayed on board along with the pilots as the jet was serviced under tight private security. All technicians who approached the plane, as well as the caterer, were photographed and carefully watched. As promised, Friar Giuseppe left to take a shower. So far as Brother Michael could see, the only weak point in this whole affair was allowing the good friar to be off alone. *Riiznor trusts him, so I must ... until proven otherwise,* Michael thought.

Friar Giuseppe returned, refreshed and in good humor. The plane door was closed, and Michael gave a nod to one of the pilots to indicate permission to take off. With only about forty-five minutes in the air, the flight between Helsinki and Joensuu would be literally a hop. The wheel chucks were removed, and the engines began their shrill whine. The spring weather was clear and sunny with little wind. Sitting down in his seat and looking out the window, Michael sighed. *It should be a smooth flight until we reach Joensuu. Then, anything can happen.*

Upon landing in Joensuu, Michael felt to make sure his Daly was snug in its holster underneath his frock and then stepped out of the plane to the waiting Mercedes. The uniformed driver was standing by the car and walked forward to greet Michael.

The driver, like Michael, was square shouldered and wore a deep tan for having been in the northern country. He also sported close-cropped hair and a short beard. His dark eyes were clear and alert.

Michael spoke first. "Cherry red."

"Blossoms are in bloom."

Michael reached out and shook the driver's

offered hand. The driver spoke with either a British or Australian accent. Michael couldn't tell which at first.

Without offering small talk, Michael asked, "Should we get started?"

"The sooner the better," the driver replied. "By the way, mate, should you care to ask, my name is Donald."

Michael gave a chuckle at this. *He must be an Aussie; he has a sense of humor. A Brit would be all business, more than likely.* As he slid into the back seat, Michael replied, "Okay, Donald. I'm Brother Michael. Glad to make your acquaintance." He barely had time to shut the car door before Donald stepped on the gas and the tires squealed in protest. Michael gave a backward glance at the plane as it stood motionless and alone. Everything was as planned ... so far.

The car phone rang. It was Riiznor. "I assume you've met and accepted Donald and that you're leaving the Joensuu airport on your way to the monastery. Is everything okay?"

"It is textbook all the way...so far anyway," Brother Michael replied.

"Donald will follow the recommended route as marked out by VI Michelin. He'll drive you directly to the Valamo Monastery, where your charges are waiting as we speak. All five charges are accounted for and cleared to come back with you. The Mercedes should have sufficient room to accommodate you all. It's approximately a four-hour round trip from Joensuu. Donald will do everything he can to assist you. Get in and out as fast as possible. I'll be in touch." There was a click, and the line went dead.

Well, it's up to us now! The show is about to start!

Michael's adrenaline pumped as he reached once again for his Daly. He glanced up just in time to see Donald give him a quick look and grin in the rearview mirror. With a nod, Michael answered the grin with one of his own.

Standing at the plane's open door, Friar Giuseppe watched as the white Mercedes pulled away from the parked aircraft. "There will be some surprises when they return," he said quietly to himself.

"I'm sorry; I didn't catch that," a voice from behind him called out.

Startled, Friar Giuseppe turned to look at the copilot, who had walked up from the lavatory. Giuseppe said, "It was nothing—just talking to myself is all."

"I do that sometimes myself," the copilot said as he headed back to his compartment. He called back over his shoulder, "There is nothing to be nervous about."

"In a minute, I'll bring you two some coffee," Giuseppe said.

Friar Giuseppe closed the hatch, reached under his habit, and pulled out his clip-fed .22 handgun. It fired high-powered, hollow-point bullets, and the stub barrel was silenced. He walked over to the coffee urn and poured two cups. He placed the cups on a silver serving tray, and then, holding the tray with one hand and the handgun with his other, he balanced the tray on top of the pointed handgun, thus partially concealing the weapon.

Friar Giuseppe took a deep breath and knocked on

the pilot's cabin door. Both men temporarily turned their heads and looked up at him as he walked in and then went back to their business—one was going over what Giuseppe assumed was a flight chart, and the other was studying what looked to be a checklist. Both were now seated with their backs to him. Without looking, the copilot reached out his hand to receive the expected cup of coffee.

There were two loud pops, and both men slumped forward. Giuseppe followed up with a head shot to each to make sure.

After slowly releasing a breath of air from between pursed lips—he hadn't realized until then that he'd been holding his breath—he turned and walked back to the passenger compartment. *Now, to concoct a story,* he thought. *Well, Yermakov said to do anything I could to slow the planned extraction down or to stop it. Replacing two pilots should take some time. Yermakov promised to tend to the legal entanglements should they arise. I wonder if murder is included in that promise.*

With that thought still in his head, Friar Giuseppe went back to the pilot's compartment, retrieved one of the cups of coffee, and gulped it down.

Donald drove fast but expertly. *Another jockey professional,* Michael thought. *Riiznor knows how and where to recruit them.* As they drove around a bend in the black tar road leading up to the long, tree-sheltered drive to Valamo's gate, Michael noticed a late-model car stopped off to the side, almost in the ditch. *That's odd.*

The vehicle seemed to catch Donald's attention as well, and Michael asked, "What do you make of it?"

"I don't like it. Warning bells are going off in my head."

"Mine too. We'll have to pay close attention to it on leaving. The only other way out is to fly out. By any chance is this car armored?"

"Sure thing, but it has its limitations."

"Well, I'm for sticking with the car. If our warning bells are right, we'll shove our guests to the floor and shoot our way out. Are you carrying anything?"

Donald gave a broad grin. "I thought you would never ask," he said as he pulled a .45 automatic pistol from beneath his uniform. "This old baby has been with me for many years and has made several checks on the bad guys."

For the first time in a long time, Brother Michael laughed. "I don't know what your background is, and I don't need to know, but I do welcome your help."

Having arrived, their white Mercedes pulled up to the stone gate of the older of the two buildings.

Donald put the limousine into drive. Brother Michael glanced at his five charges: Dr. Perez and her assistant, Neal; Kola's former head engineer and project manager, Rostikov; the former drilling foreman, Rantanen, who guarded the vial; and Father Dominick. Michael pondered about his guests. *Interesting—one*

lone Spanish American woman, one American, two Russians, and wherever the frocked Dominick came from. Being well read, Michael remembered the ancient Roman joke: "What happens when you put a Jew, a Roman, and a Briton alone on an island? The Jew will build a temple, the Roman will build a fort, and the Briton will start a fight." *However, what happens when you put two Russians, two Americans, and two men of the Catholic cloth in the back of an automobile?* Michael chuckled.

As they neared the bend after exiting the long drive to the monastery, Donald accelerated. The lone car still sat beside the road. Donald called Michael's attention to it.

"I don't like it," Michael called out from the back of the car. After a quick hesitation, he told the group to get down and cover their heads. "This is just precautionary," he said.

"Aren't you being too cautious?" Neal asked. "I think we should—"

Before he could finish his statement, an explosion rocked the Mercedes. Donald fought the steering wheel to keep the big car on the road.

"Gun it!" Michael yelled.

Gunshots rang out, and the right front tire blew apart. The Mercedes swerved into a shallow ditch and came to a sudden halt, threatening to topple over. As Michael dove out of the car, he caught a glimpse of where the shooting was coming from and returned fire. Shots were coming from behind him, from the hood on the driver's side. *Donald must be out and returning fire.*

Everything went quiet. Seconds later a motorcycle could be heard speeding off into the distance. Both Donald and Michael continued firing toward the sound of the motorcycle engine. The noise became fainter.

Donald called out, "He's leaving us!"

"Wait a moment! It might be a trap!"

The two slowly stood up. Michael looked back at his charges, who began to move from the floor of the vehicle. Only four heads appeared where there should have been five. Jennifer screamed.

"Oh shit!" Michael exclaimed as he ran back to their car. "Who's hurt?" Then he looked in at the priest slumped in the corner of the back seat. Blood trickled down the man's face and onto his priestly collar. Michael reached for the man's wrist to see if he could find a pulse. There was none. "He must have waited too long to get his head down," Michael whispered. "He probably wanted to see his flock safe first. A gentleman to the end."

Michael crossed himself as he pulled out his cell phone to call Riiznor for instructions and assistance. Jennifer started to cry. Neal put his arm around her shoulders while Stefan stared blankly at the body. Surgey said nothing, just shook his head.

After hanging up with Riiznor, Michael used his gun to gesture Donald toward him. They walked past the shot-up auto and into some heavy foliage to where they thought the shooter had been positioned.

"One didn't make it, huh?" Donald asked.

"No, the priest took a shot right into his temple."

They found the upturned earth where the cycle had spun its wheel in its escape.

"Aha, look here," Donald said as he pointed to some blood dripping off a leaf from a tree. "We must have winged him, at least bad enough to make him retreat. That's probably why the shooting stopped suddenly."

Michael said as he came up behind Donald, "I suppose if we dig around enough in the grass, we'll find shell casings. But it's not necessary. I pretty much know who we're up against."

The two looked at each other in confirmation. Michael took a long look at Donald and said, "I suspect you've been briefed as much I have."

Donald replied with a broad grin. "You think we actually got lucky and wounded this Karpov?"

Michael laughed as his cell phone rang. It was Friar Giuseppe.

"Michael, there has been an accident!"

"Define 'accident'!" Michael commanded.

"I know you told me to be vigilant, but while I was in the lavatory, our pilots were both shot! I heard some popping sounds but didn't think anything was seriously wrong—perhaps just the jet engines cooling down. I came out of the lavatory and went straight to the pilot's compartment and found them both slumped over, dead. Someone had to have come on board as I was taking care of business. What do you want me to do?"

"Don't leave the plane. I'll call the control tower and notify Riiznor. Just stay put!" Michael growled. "One more question, good Friar Giuseppe: If you thought it was just the engines cooling down, why did you immediately go to the pilot's cabin? I'm going to want some serious answers from you in person. You stay on that damn plane till I get there."

Watching Michael, Donald sensed something else had gone wrong but held his peace and waited.

Not attempting to conceal anything from Donald, Michael immediately called the control tower and asked for security.

The security officer in charge was dumbfounded. "That can't be. We've had your jet under camera surveillance, as explicitly instructed, and absolutely no one has come near the plane. I can guarantee it."

"Well, call the authorities and start an investigation from your end. Impound the plane, but leave the luggage alone. I'll retrieve it."

Michael rang off and quickly dialed Riiznor again.

After listening to Michael, Riiznor said, "Don't go back to the plane. Take the limo and head straight for Helsinki after you leave Dominick's remains in the hands of the monks at Valamo. I'll have another private jet waiting for you there in Helsinki. Don't worry about the luggage. It will be taken care of. Your remaining passengers are of the utmost importance."

"What about Friar Giuseppe?" Michael asked.

"Something doesn't smell right. At this point we can't take our chances with Giuseppe's explanation—we don't have time to figure out who is telling the truth. From here on, he is my problem, not yours. Anything else?"

"Yeah, your Donald is a good man with a gun!"

"There is nothing like hedging one's bets."

With the conclusion of the call, Michael and Donald hurried back to their car. They had to get it out of the ditch, fix it, and get back on the road.

Donald stood in the Helsinki Airport's public viewing lounge and watched the Vatican's chartered jet lift off the runway with its very important cargo.

His cell phone rang. It was Riiznor. "Excellent work! Now, drive back to Joensuu and have a talk with Giuseppe—that is, if you can find him. I've been informed that he has left the impounded jet, and his exact whereabouts are unknown. If you find him alive, bring him back to Rome. I want to conduct the interrogation personally. If the mob gets to him first, he'll vanish—and not to his liking either. Whether he knows it or not, Giuseppe is a member of the walking dead. The Mafia doesn't appreciate loose ends. Do you have any questions?"

"No, sir. I'll find him if he's still walking. The old Mercedes is holding up well, but it does need attention, especially some bodywork. The back window is out, and there are telltale holes along one side. How about I pick out a body shop and leave it, and you contact them to confirm and decide? I'll pick up a rental to drive back to Joensuu. Once in Joensuu, I'll find a room downtown and see what I can dig up."

"Sounds good! Report back to me as soon as you find some living space to work from. I want Giuseppe back here if possible. A certain priest personally recommended him to me for special assignments. I must sit this individual down and have a little conversation with him before you get back. I thought I was running a tight operation, but there may be some leaks."

After a pause, Donald said, "If I bring him back, our Friar Giuseppe may have a few bruises on his person, but he will be able to talk. Any problem with that?"

"None whatsoever."

Cardinal Riiznor ended the call, and Donald stood there for a moment looking down at his cell phone. *What a remarkable invention,* he mused.

After working a kink out of his neck with his palm, Donald went looking for the nearest lunch counter. He muttered, "I get fed, and then the car gets attention—first things first."

It was raining and late afternoon when Donald Cotton left the outskirts of Helsinki in a two-door, cream-colored Daihatsu rental. Rivulets of water appeared and disappeared on the hood of the car as the windshield wipers beat a steady rhythm on the windshield. The radio played a soft rock tune, and Donald tapped the beat on the steering wheel, humming along as he went. There was no mention yet in the broadcast of a possible international problem. Donald never liked inventing problems when there were none. Imagination could really help in solving known problems, but it could also lead one down unnecessary paths of dead ends. He decided to enjoy a few moments of peace while he could.

Once in Joensuu, he decided he would stay at the hotel Atrium—a three-star hotel located in the heart of the city with reasonable rates. The current rate was posted at eighty-nine US dollars per night for a single, and the rooms were clean and comfortable. The location was good too, for the hotel was situated just before the bridge on Siltakatu Street—a main thoroughfare that would take him to the train depot and the other half of Joensuu. Almost all the likely spots—churches and bars alike—that Friar Giuseppe might run to would be within walking distance. The Atrium would make a good base of operations from which to hunt down the little shit in or out of his priestly garb. If the Russian mob got to him first, that was Giuseppe's bad luck.

MISSED DETAIL

The air conditioner hummed as Peter sat at his desk in Washington, DC, playing with his pewter nameplate. It was a gift from his sister and had "Peter Alfred Wentworth" emblazoned in gold across the front. The day ahead loomed empty, much the same as the rest of his life at present.

"Your next assignment, Peter!" Richard Jacoby called out as he entered with a small folder tucked under his arm and a grin on his face. With a loud slap, the folder landed on Peter's desk, causing a few notes to flutter to the floor.

"Oh, another job?" Peter asked casually, failing to hide his lack of concern and his irritation over the scattering of his papers. "When did this come through?"

"Just yesterday."

Peter picked it up and perused through it. "I wondered how long it would take before I drew an assignment in Africa ... and Kenya of all places."

"You haven't heard the worst of it yet. For cover, you'll be traveling with missionaries as a journalist."

"No shit? Who's to be my lucky target?"

"Edward Frenchette, an arms dealer. It seems he

has expanded his operations to include drugs. This is to be a favor to the Brits, as they are responsible for having spawned him. This is a political embarrassment for both the English and Kenyan governments."

"Why me, and why can't some of the locals nail him?"

"In brief, you are one of our best, and that's what's required for this job. You're not presently assigned either, I might also add. The job should be done quickly, and not be traceable to anyone or any country. To be sure, for the sake of appearances, the local authorities will go through the motions of an investigation. So, in the end, that means we get to do this to uphold the veil of plausible deniability for the Brits. Therefore, you, my friend, must step in and give a helping hand to our friendly neighbors."

"My weekend plans are shot! No pun intended. Damn it! So...when do I leave?"

"Your full briefing will be at four this afternoon, and you'll catch a flight to New York in the morning."

"I'll barely have time for a cup of coffee."

"I think you've got the picture. Good luck, and report immediately back to me when you return to Washington ... and, Peter, I mean immediately. There is special interest in this matter, from people way higher than my pay grade."

"Isn't there always? Oh, what's my code name on this misadventure?"

"Mr. Jack Armstrong, as it's explained in the folder."

"Jack Armstrong, the all-American, I can't wait," Peter mockingly replied as Jacoby exited his office.

An attractive brunette flight attendant leaned over and handed Peter his favorite aspirin cocktail, which consisted of two aspirins and a glass of 7 Up with bitters. His window seat on the current 1987 jetliner was just ahead of the right wing. It always made him nervous to look down and watch the trembling engine pod as it hung suspended beneath the wing.

"Damn if that thing doesn't fall off one day," he muttered to himself.

He was starting to unwind and come off the adrenaline that he had been on for some forty-odd hours. His side ached. Montoobo had gone too far, and now he was out of the grand picture of human events. Peter wondered what Jacoby's response was going to be. Sleep began to win the fight as he gazed at the flight attendant's retreating figure. She stopped and bent over another passenger, revealing a rather shapely pair of legs.

He thought of another pair of attractive brown legs. *I didn't mean to take her out, damn it!* Peter's thoughts were assailing him as he drifted off to sleep. His conscience was nagging him, as it usually did when he was very tired and alone with his thoughts. *How did it happen that a young, churchgoing boy ended up being a state-run hired gun? Am I going to shoot people for the rest of my life?*

On the final approach to the airport, Peter could see the exposed city of Nairobi with its rectangular and cylindrical high-rises unnaturally jutting out of the surrounding landscape. Once outside the city's tentacles, though, one would be in flat, sprawling bush country.

The jet landed and taxied up to the arrival gate. Moments later, Peter collected his luggage and headed for the nearest exit.

"Would a Mr. Jack Armstrong please report to the operations desk of the blue concourse for an important message?" a voice over the loudspeaker system called out in English.

When Peter made it to the operations desk, a man with a rich baritone voice and an Oxford English accent said, "Ah, Mr. Armstrong. Welcome to Nairobi, the heartbeat of East Africa." Dressed in an exquisitely tailored suit, it was none other than Mr. Montoobo, head of Kenya's political right wing.

"My people will be assisting you on this very delicate mission of yours." He leaned in close to Peter. "You know, of course, that Mr. Edward Frenchette has to go."

If this turkey knows about it, half the African dominion knows, Peter thought.

"Hello, Montoobo! What a surprise to find you here," Peter replied, masking his contempt.

"I have taken it upon myself to escort you to the Commodore Hotel to meet Mr. Tobey. As already explained to you, Mr. Tobey will be your cover, as he heads the missionary troop that is establishing itself here in Nairobi. You and I will talk later about our mutual problem," Montoobo said as they walked toward a waiting black four-door Mercedes.

A tiny epoxy bowl filled with concentrated sulfuric acid was now anchored to the copper tubing that carried natural gas to the burner of Frenchette's stove. A hole in the bottom of the bowl allowed the bubbling acid to slowly drip down and eat at the exposed copper surface. Once the acid ate its way through the tubing, the piped-in gas would be released to the interior of the apartment. The pilot light would go out, but that would not be noticed under the shiny enamel stove top. The sulfuric acid would take approximately two and a half hours to eat its way through. It would take another one and a half hours before the escaping gas would become noticeable. By that time, Frenchette would be in the middle of his late-afternoon nap. Intel from Montoobo's three weeks of surveillance had proved Frenchette's rigidity in his daily routines.

"Why Washington agreed to cooperate with Montoobo I'll never know," Peter said quietly to himself. He was stationed in a second-floor sleeping room across the narrow alley from Frenchette's apartment.

Frenchette was loaded with end-user certificates, necessary in the international sale of arms, while Montoobo was strictly African politics. With a little guidance, Peter felt that certain governments could have made effective use of Frenchette and his contacts, but Montoobo was strictly a political liability with no redeeming social value.

At his window, Peter waited. He had a 9 mm Mauser fitted with an ignition cap that would explode on impact and ignite the accumulating gas in Frenchette's apartment. Everything would be consumed in the explosion and resulting blaze. There should be no traces left. His wristwatch showed 5:00 p.m., which meant there'd been time enough to allow sufficient gas to fill Frenchette's rooms. Peter took careful aim. Looking down the elongated silenced barrel, he gently squeezed the trigger. A heartbeat later he felt the heat and the force of the blast through his open window. The sound of the explosion echoed off the surrounding buildings, followed by the tinkling of broken glass from shattered windows falling to the ground below.

"Goodbye, Mr. Chips!" Peter muttered, remembering a movie he had once seen starring Peter O'Toole.

He had thoroughly cleaned the apartment beforehand while wearing rubber gloves, and he'd still been wearing the thin gloves when he'd squeezed the trigger. Peter packed the Mauser, tucked it under his coat, removed the gloves, and made for the hall, which led to the street in front. The wailing of sirens began to drown out the screams of people showered in the falling glass. A crowd started gathering to watch the blazing second-floor apartment as flames licked the outside of the complex.

Once outside, Peter stood in the crowd for a moment and watched the fire and then made for his parked vehicle. Montoobo's people had acquired the car for him and then made sure it would not be blocked before he made his escape with it. Peter had to get back to the Commodore to establish himself with the missionaries. He was thirsting for a cool soda and a couple of aspirins.

As Peter drove toward the Nairobi suburb where the Commodore Hotel was located, he noticed that the fuel gauge was only on three-fourths of a tank. *What the hell!* That morning he'd checked all fluid levels and topped off the petrol himself. There was no reason for the tank to show anything but full, especially after being parked for most of the day.

Damn Montoobo and his bunch. They had to have been screwing around while I was in the room tending to details, Peter guessed. He shifted down and parked on a secluded side street. *Montoobo got his work done; now he wants to remove me.*

Peter got out of the car, taking the packed Mauser with him. He didn't bother with anything else, because something told him the car was going to explode anyway. If he'd judged wrong, he was in trouble, for he was leaving traceable evidence behind.

When Peter had walked about three hundred yards, the little car disappeared in a tremendous explosion. Just as he'd thought. The blast almost rivaled the explosion in Frenchette's apartment. Peter continued walking, putting distance between himself and the burning auto before local authorities could make their appearance with their familiar wailing sirens. He was forced to walk back to the Commodore, for fear hailing a cab might raise questions from some of the locals.

In the game of hide and seek, the bag of tricks included removing gasoline from an auto tank and inserting a canister-type grenade with a rubber band holding the trigger lever instead of the normal pin. There was an *x* amount of time before the gasoline ate away the rubber band and released the lever. Based on Peter's experiences, this was likely how Montoobo's people had pulled it off. If he were an inexperienced assassin, they would have succeeded. But, damn it, they'd made the mistake of hiring the best. Now payback!

In the hotel lobby of the Commodore, Mr. Tobey was waiting up for Peter. Mr. Tobey was paunchy, middle-aged, and constantly wiping the sweat from his brow. However, he did have a pleasing personality and the reputation of being a good organizer.

After a pause, he said, "Well, Mr. Armstrong, I know it's late, but I wanted to go over the itinerary with you for tomorrow ... I want you to take a couple of shots as we set up our medical tents."

Shooting was exactly what Peter had in mind, but not the kind Mr. Tobey was expecting.

"Can we do this tomorrow, say around midmorning? Something has just recently come up, and I have to run an important errand first thing in the morning," Peter said.

Mr. Tobey hesitated but agreed, since he needed some time himself to catch up on financial reports for the missionary council back in Georgia.

"Great," said Peter, knowing full well he would not be in Nairobi when Mr. Tobey came looking for him.

Up in his hotel room, Peter rang the airport for the first available flight out of Nairobi. The first flight was to Paris at 7:00 a.m. with a one-hour stopover in Cairo. He took it. Peter would leave it to Jacoby to explain his absence to Mr. Tobey. This was Jacoby's mess anyway. He wondered how long it would take Montoobo's bunch to realize that there was no body in the burned-out car.

It had been a long day, and he needed a hot shower and some fresh clothes.

It was now two in the morning. After dressing, Peter screwed the silencer back on his gun and listened at the door. There wasn't a sound. He gently opened the door and checked down the long corridor. Nobody in sight. They were not on to him yet.

Outside a soft rain was falling, and the heat of the previous day had dissipated. Peter knew where Montoobo was most likely to be. His sexual appetite was well known in certain circles, and his current mistress was most accommodating.

A cab took Peter to within two blocks of Montoobo's mistress's dwelling. He would walk the remaining distance.

The little bungalow was hidden within the night shadows, but there was just enough moonlight to distinguish large objects.

There were neither guards nor guard dogs. *The bastard is struck with overconfidence.*

Peter went around to the screened-in back door, just off from what he surmised to be the bedroom. There was still no sign of guards. He pulled out the silenced Mauser and released the safety catch. Holding the weapon firmly in his right hand, he opened the back door with a gentle pry.

Peter entered and within moments found what looked to be the bedroom door. He gave it a slight nudge. A shot rang out. A blow to his left side spun him backward, tumbling. He turned as he hit the floor, firing. He heard a gasp and then a crash as if a lamp had smashed to the floor. Two more shots came from behind the door. Wood splinters hit him in the face and neck, but the trajectory of the shots luckily missed him entirely. Maneuvering to a prone position, he fired repeatedly back at the door, placing each shot below the preceding one. He heard a cry and a thud, as if a body had fallen. Silence followed.

Peter lay motionless as he sucked in air. Pain radiated throughout his torso with each breath. Rolling over onto his right side while still holding his gun, he reached down and brushed his painful ribs—hot, sticky, and wet. It hurt to breathe.

"Miserable bastard!" he yelled.

Peter fired another low shot through the bedroom door in anger. This time there was no return fire. He continued to lie motionless, trying to determine how badly he was hit. His left rib cage throbbed with lancing pain. Blood oozed but didn't spout, indicating a flesh wound. *The bullet probably just grazed the ribs and kept going,* he thought. He could live with that, literally.

Peter crawled over to what was left of the bedroom door and pushed it open with the barrel of his gun. Retrieving a penlight from a pants pocket, he quickly scanned the room. A naked young woman lay with her head and left arm hanging over the side of the bed. A table lamp, or what was left of it, lay in pieces on the floor close to her. There was no movement from her, nor would there ever be again. Blood was dripping down the side of her still face.

Peter flicked the light over to where Montoobo lay

on the floor. Judging from the smell of stale booze, there had to be some open bottles nearby. He crawled to Montoobo and rolled him over. Peter held the gun to Montoobo's temple as he placed a finger to the man's neck. A faint pulse indicated that Montoobo was yet alive.

"A tough bird, aren't you?" Peter whispered. "Thanks for trying to have me killed. Your people should pay closer attention to details." Peter moved the barrel's silencer closer to Montoobo's right temple and pulled the trigger.

He carefully stood to minimize the pain knifing from his side with every minor movement, walked back around to the foot of the bed, and gently touched the woman's ankle. Peter marveled at her beautifully shaped calf and ankle. Under different circumstances, he would have gone after her himself, for she was a beautiful woman. For once, he and Montoobo agreed on something. Peter had to laugh, albeit painfully. The guilt would come later, as it usually did, in cases such as this.

Peter slowly blinked his eyelids. He'd evidently fallen asleep. The stewardess nudged his arm and explained that she had an incoming call from Washington for a Mr. Peter Wentworth.

Peter looked up at her in disbelief. "How the hell did they know I was on this flight?"

"I'm sorry, sir; I can't answer that. But will you take the call?"

After a pause, he said, "I'll take it … Is there somewhere I can talk in private?"

"You'll have to take it at the booth, sir."

Peter went and picked up the receiver in the small stand-up cubicle. Not waiting for the caller to identify himself, he said, "Richard, you son of a bitch! How did you know I was on this flight?"

"Now calm down. We do have our methods, don't we?" came the reply.

"You know what? I had to also eliminate Montoobo and ended up killing his very lovely girlfriend along with him. You know what else? I'm not sure I can work for you anymore. I've just about had it!" With that, Peter slammed down the receiver, grimacing in pain as he did so. Holding his self-taped left side, he walked back to his seat and what was left of his aspirin cocktail and life. It was entirely possible that it had been in their plans all along for him to eliminate Montoobo. *Have I've been duped? Their number one?*

He muttered under his breath as he returned to his seat, "Oh, I'll report back all right. I want some questions answered as well."

MY QUEEN

"Chip a hole here," Kelicia commanded as she pointed toward the marks on the top of the exposed skull of the still, lifeless body of Queen Boudica. The head had been previously shaven, and a patch of skin approximately four inches in diameter had been cut and peeled away, with the remaining edge of skin singed and crispy. The incense candles weren't sufficient to cover the acrid, gagging odor of decaying flesh and burnt hair.

With the moon now entering its fullness, Kelicia, a Druid sorceress, removed herself from earthly bounds.

I dare not interrupt her, I thought.

"The first tapping hole has to be the width of a hand above the brow and centered between the eyes. The remaining three holes will be on both sides and centered in back. I will cut along the line connecting the holes," the sorceress said. She looked deep into the eyes of her attendant, who held the instruments, wanting to make sure he understood her instructions as he began tapping the holes. There could be no slips now. Everything hung on the results. Per custom, if she failed, Kelicia would be lying beside the queen in death.

The slightest air current in the room was cool to Kelicia's naked body, resulting in a wave of small hairs standing on end. Then she turned her hypnotic gaze upon me. I took a couple of steps back. My hand instinctively reached for the hilt of my sword. I, Drustanus, was the field commander of Queen Boudica's light chariot and cavalry force. I'd been a veteran of many campaigns and had fought both with and against the Romans for my queen, whose body lay still before me. Many sights I had witnessed, but none to match the scene that faced me now.

Her attendant removed the top of the skull, exposing the brain cavity, to which salt water was then added. Strips of lead and copper were gently inserted into opposite sides of the brain cavity. When finished, Kelicia stepped up and took hold of the exposed ends of the two inserted strips, copper in one hand and lead in the other. While she held the ends, two female attendants vigorously massaged her naked body with a flaxlike material to produce a static jolt.

A rhythmic drumbeat replaced the silence as the sorceress's body began to sway under the efforts of the female attendants. A polished metallic mirror was held under the nostrils of the prostrated queen.

My knees felt weak as an awkward thought occurred to me. *What should I say to a queen who has been dead for three days and then arises? Do I give her a battle report?*

I had witnessed our queen fall surrounded by Romans. A glinting ax had been raised for a final deathblow when an arrow whined over my shoulder. The wielder of the ax had toppled to the ground as the bolt hit its mark. It had been a rallying point for us, and we'd stormed to where she lay. My troops had fought like demons to reclaim her body from the Ninth Legion. The Romans would have taken her back to Rome as a trophy, dragging her, dead or otherwise, through the streets of Rome in a triumphal procession if they'd been successful. This could not be allowed.

I wanted to blame Nero for the recent wars and this tragedy, but he was but a fool. It was Lucius Seneca, the power behind the throne, who was responsible for the change in attitudes of the Romans toward the Iceni tribe and vice versa. Wasn't it just a few short years ago that Queen Boudica had accepted an invitation from Emperor Claudius to receive his son Britannicus? The plan had been for Britannicus to continue his maturation as a royal guest of the queen and her husband, King Prasutagus. Queen Boudica had suspected that Claudius wanted Britannicus away from the intrigues of Rome and Claudius's current wife, Agrippina.

I held my queen's judgment in high respect. My devotion to her was what had brought me here to this cave, in the slim hope she would be returned to us in some way.

The drumbeat ceased. The sorceress stopped her swaying, and her sweating body became rigid and her gaze transfixed. I remained motionless, as if welded to the damp, dark floor. My chest heaved with short and rapid shallow breaths. All my muscles grew taut as tension filled my body.

By gods! There was fog on the polished mirror, and a familiar voice gasped out in a barely audible pitch, "I hurt! I hurt!" The queen's chest convulsed, and her body jerked. And then all was still. The fog on the mirror disappeared.

It took a few moments to digest what had happened. I knew Suetonius Paulinus and his Roman legions were fast approaching due to scouting reports. Suetonius would be only too happy to put the whole damn bunch of us to the sword. The thought occurred to me that maybe I should save him the trouble and put the sorceress and her entourage to the sword myself.

I broke loose from my inertia and walked over to the sorceress while everyone else remained rooted. Her eyes were glazed and unfocused. I slapped her across the face and shook her slender shoulders to bring her back to the moment. Her sweating body was warm to the touch and pliant in my hands.

"Kelicia, the queen is dead. However, it seemed as if she did come back to us ... for a fleeting moment anyway."

Her eyes started to focus, and she seemed to grasp what I was saying. "I did it then? You won't kill me?" she asked in a rasping whisper.

"Yes, you did it, and no, I won't kill you." Softening my voice, I said, "Now listen. Wrap the queen as quickly as you can. There is a wagon outside hooked up to a horse. I want you and the queen's body on that wagon fast. We have little time to spare." Turning to my first officer, I called out, "Clear the mob!"

The night shadows were receding, and the early-morning breeze carried hope for escape as we exited the cave. There was a cool dampness in the air as the morning mist rose from the moors. The queen's body had been wrapped hastily for burial. I needed Kelicia's help in this, for I could not bring myself to touch the queen. In my imagination, spurred by fatigue and probably superstition, I feared she would come alive again if I were to. I did not want to relive that sight. The sorceress would have to bury her.

Kelicia climbed up beside me as I took the reins and spurred my horse, which was tethered to the wagon. I had the equivalent of a cohort with me, mounted and spread out in a column of twos, positioned both in front and behind me. However, we were no match for a well-fed, disciplined rank of Roman troops, cavalry or otherwise. My men and I had not eaten or slept in two days. Flight was our immediate agenda in hopes of avoiding contact with Paulinus's advanced skirmishers.

As our column moved forward, the noise of conflict was heard coming from our front, where the lead was just out of sight due to the underbrush alongside the winding path.

"No ... no ... not now," I said, half out loud.

"What is it?" Kelicia asked, turning her head toward me.

"That, sorceress, is the sound of battle," I said. "It's got to be more than just the sweeping away of a few skirmishers."

I turned the wagon halfway around in the middle of the road, gave the order to hold the front if possible, and took off through the underbrush.

Only ten mounted auxiliaries with sword and bow followed me.

The forest immediately closed around us, and Kelicia became increasingly nervous. The Druids' sacred oak trees formed a canopy over our reduced funeral procession, and the occasional rabbit scuttled out of our way. There was not a breath of wind, and shadows lurked behind every tree. I was too tired to heed anything.

Kelicia lightly touched my shoulder and whispered, "This is sacred Druid ground."

I was beyond care. *Surely the Druids would not begrudge our intrusion in attempting to find the valiant queen a peaceful resting place,* I thought.

After traveling some distance through the woods, leading the way with the wagon, we topped a knoll. As we descended at speed down the backside of the knoll, wagon and horse came to an abrupt halt, almost throwing both Kelicia and me over the horse's rump. After recovering, I gave the horse a whip. It struggled as it started to sink. It was then I felt the wagon lowering into the earth.

"Bog!" Kelicia screamed as mud began to ooze up around the wagon's sides and wheels.

My small band that followed quickly halted and dismounted while still on firm ground. They quickly threw a makeshift rope of vines and reins out to us.

"Lie flat, hang on, and don't struggle!" my auxiliary officer shouted to me.

With heroic effort from my men, we were pulled to firm land. Kelicia stood shivering and caked in mud, watching the horses, wagon, and contents sink into the morass. The harnessed horse and my tethered mount didn't have a chance. Their cries still echoed in my mind. An eerie silence descended as we watched the bog claim its royal prize. Kelicia made a sign as the wagon and its load disappeared forever. The only fanfare was the stark, strident cry of a raven. The ancient isle had claimed the queen as its own.

I put my arms around Kelicia to comfort her. Shaking, she laid her head on my shoulder. She started to cry as she clung to me. Though a sorceress, Kelicia was a woman, after all. Everything that had happened in the last few hours was more than enough for anyone.

"My queen," I whispered, "it's yours for the taking."

Kelicia must have heard me, for she stiffened and raised her head up erect.

Breaking the moment of recognition, a young officer of the auxiliary whispered over to me, "Sir, I'll put a watch out and see if we can scrounge up something to eat. If there is a bog, there is a river close by, and if there is a river, there is fish."

I nodded in agreement. "We'll camp here for the remainder of the day and hope for the best tomorrow, if we survive the night."

Looking at Kelicia, I could almost see a resemblance to Boudica in her begrimed face. Standing in a clearing, the sun seemed to open as it spread its warmth over our small assembly.

SLIP SLIDING AWAY

On the night of March 18, 1990, two thieves disguised as police officers entered Boston's Isabella Stewart Gardner Museum. They trussed two guards and made off with three paintings by Rembrandt, five by Degas, one by Manet, and one of only thirty-six known in existence by Vermeer. At an estimated total value of $200 million, it may have been the most lucrative art theft in history.

A few years later, Gretta looked out the window at the overcast morning sky. It was the twenty-fifth of October. Rain was again forecast for the late afternoon and evening. It had been raining off and on for the past three days. *What a dismal day to do such a dismal job,* she thought. The telephone rang.

"Are you going to talk to him tonight then?" the familiar voice of Steven Jackson asked in a conspiratorial tone.

"Yes ... Please don't ask me anymore. It's not exactly

easy telling your husband your marriage is over. So don't push me!"

"Sorry. I'll call you tomorrow."

"Listen! I'm picking Howard up at the train station this evening and driving him to our club. Over dinner and a glass of wine, I'm going to lay the cards on the table. I think he'll understand. Yes, call me tomorrow at my office ... say around four. By the way, what exactly are you doing tonight?"

"I'm transferring some artwork ... finishing a job. You know I love you!" Steven said and promptly hung up the receiver.

Gretta heard the click. *Everything has its price, and nothing is free, including love ... whatever that is,* she thought.

Gretta glanced at her wristwatch. It was six, and the rainy sky was growing dark. She downshifted and rounded the wet hairpin curve at sixty miles per hour in her classic black 1958 Triumph. Howard reflexively grabbed the dash-mounted handgrip even though he wore a seat belt, as did she.

"Aren't you driving a bit fast? We have all evening."

"I told the maître d' we'd be there by seven. He's holding a table for us that overlooks the river."

Gretta ignored Howard's growing anxiety over her driving as she stared through continually sweeping wiper blades. The rain squall was gaining momentum. She hit the accelerator on the straightaway.

"Look! You don't have to hurry! Can't you slow

down? Besides, I can't believe you want to eat out on a night like this anyway."

Gretta and Howard Burkman had been married for six seemingly endless years, and Gretta felt she was on the threshold of a whole new life if she could make Howard understand. His train had been an hour late, and she was driving fast to make up for lost time. Raining or not, she was determined to arrive at the club at a reasonable time, so they could eat and have the discussion.

Of all nights to be late! Gretta thought as she shot him a sideways glance. Her speed approached eighty miles per hour on the straightaways, but she reluctantly braked and downshifted again for the next curve. The engine whined.

She clutched and again shifted gears. The rear wheels lost their traction on the wet pavement, and the little Triumph started to drift into a skid. The tail end of the vehicle broke loose as she fought the wheel, attempting to steer into the skid. Howard clung to the dash grip. With grim determination, Gretta continued fighting the steering wheel as she tried to keep the little car on the road.

When the right front tire hit the side gravel, the car did a complete spin and landed in a shallow ditch with the rear embedded in a fresh mixture of mud and coarse field grass. The sharply turned front wheels clung to the top edge of the ditch. The engine was still running as exhaust forced its way through the churned morass.

Gretta sat with her head bent down over the steering wheel, shaking. Howard was also trembling.

"You should turn the ignition off," He said in a choked voice.

Gretta barely heard him over the ringing in her head. With a quivering hand, she reached over and turned the ignition off. The engine sputtered, then died. Howard opened his door against a brace of mud. After inhaling a deep lungful of night air, he clambered over the uprooted earth and went around to her side of the car.

"You don't have to help me. I'm all right," Gretta said shortly. She pushed her door open, turned her body around, and planted her feet in the mud. Her trembling legs wouldn't support her, and she fell back into the auto. Howard grabbed her by the arms and pulled her up onto the wet pavement.

"I think we'll have to walk the rest of the way," he said gently as he wiped the dripping strands of hair out of her eyes. "We are in a mess, aren't we?"

Her lower lip was quivering. She gave a nod and looked mournfully down the long, dark stretch of highway. This wasn't the plan. *It was supposed to be short and sweet. Meet, have a few drinks, end our marriage, and back by midnight.* Rain continued to fall. Gretta was soaked, and her cold skirt clung to her slender, five-foot-four body. Howard at least wore a jacket and could turn the collar up. There wasn't another pair of headlights in sight.

Howard went down to the car and pulled out a blanket they had used on more-pleasant afternoons. He put the blanket over her shoulders, and they started to walk in the steady rain.

After walking for an hour and a half, Gretta's teeth

chattered from the cold. In the surrounding darkness off to his right, Howard thought he saw a silhouette of what looked like a barn.

"Gretta, look over there. We really do need to get out of the rain. Do you think it could give us shelter?"

Both wet and cold from the pelting rain, Gretta and Howard walked over and looked up at the large, shadowed building that stood before them. They could just make out some of the splintered edges of wood and the rough stone masonry that supported the old wooden frame. The smell of manure and rotting hay filled their nostrils as the wind and rain whipped around the dark, foreboding structure.

"We're a long way from a candlelit dinner," Howard whispered. He began to feel edgy and tense.

"Listen ..." She shushed him. "Do you hear something?" Fear crawled up her back.

Gretta turned, and in the darkness, she got a glimpse of Howard's normally rugged frame crumpling like a rag doll. As she tried to scream, Gretta felt a tremendous blow to her side. The world began to tumble. All sights, sounds, and feelings quickly disappeared into blackness.

Gretta felt a throbbing pain in the back of her head and neck as she lay motionless. She blinked her eyes to clear her mind and orient herself. She tried to focus but could see nothing in the darkness. She shivered in her wet clothes and tried to move but could not. She raised her head, but it hurt. She let out a gasp of pain and allowed her head to fall back into the hay. The odor of wet, rotting hay permeated the darkness. Gretta could hear heavy, labored breathing not far from her. She hoped it was Howard. *Please, God, let it be Howard!*

From the darkness came a rasping voice. "Did you tie them good?" Not waiting for a reply, the man said, "Damn it! What else can go wrong tonight? Besides the truck being late and this damn rain, now we have a couple of idiots on our hands. I tell you, after tonight's job, I'm through with this shitty mess!"

Another man replied derisively, "You're damn right! After tonight's pickup, there will be no paintings left. You will be through!"

The two cursed the cold, the rain, and their forced abduction of two witnesses who had turned up out of nowhere. The past years of stress and liquor had dulled their senses.

Off to one corner of the damp, dimly lit room, a painting was propped against the wall. It was Jan Vermeer's *The Concert*, which had been painted sometime between 1665 and 1666. Besides the damage incurred from being hacked off its stretcher at the museum in haste, it now showed dirt and water stains as well. The thieves had grown negligent over time and familiarity.

Gretta tried to lift her head again but could only give a low moan due to the pain. The voices of the two individuals had come from somewhere behind where she lay. She tried to move her arms and legs again but couldn't, and then she understood why. As her mental fog lifted, she realized both her ankles and wrists were tied. In her awakening awareness, she realized that it might be best not to call attention to herself and just lie as still as she possibly could. Her head continued to throb, and she felt nauseous. She prayed Howard would stay quiet and not challenge their abductors.

"I think I hear the truck," the rasping voice called out from the other side of the hay mound.

"Looks like it. Don't say a word about our two ... guests. After the transfer is complete and we've been paid, I'll explain the situation to the boss. I have half a mind not to tell him anything. We could just leave the two tied and let the rats have them. Their remains won't be found for months. The more I think about it, go back and gag them! As far as I'm concerned, they did themselves in!"

Oh no, thought Gretta, *I'll strangle in my own vomit.* She saw a beam of light come over the top of the hay and shut her eyes, pretending to be unconscious. Rough hands grabbed her by the throat and forced her head back. Calloused fingers opened her mouth, and a slimy, gritty cloth was shoved over her tongue and into her throat. She struggled for breath. Strong hands squeezed her breasts and stroked her abdomen. With eyes still closed, Gretta tried to ignore the hands and concentrated on breathing through her nose to prevent choking.

Wooden doors creaked from the other side of the hay. Fuel-laden exhaust fumes filled the air as a truck backed into the musty barn.

Gretta felt the hands pull away. She refused to open her eyes and braced herself for what she thought would be the inevitable tearing of her clothes. She waited for what seemed like an eternity. Nothing happened. Gretta opened her eyes slowly. The man was gone.

"Where's the painting?" a voice called out, followed by the slamming of a vehicle door.

Gretta's eyes opened wide in horror. She recognized that voice. It sounded like Steven's. She remembered Steven had mentioned something about transferring some art during their earlier telephone conversation.

Dressed in denim coveralls, the two newcomers lowered a ramp from the back of the truck. Steven gave the command to load the painting.

"I've got it," the man with the raspy voice replied as he picked up the heavily damaged Vermeer and started up the ramp. There was a great deal of mud clinging to the bottom of his boots, oozing out from between the cleats. Halfway up the ramp, he lost traction on the ramp's grating. He fell, twisting as he did so. The miscreant landed on top of the painting, punching a hole through the skirted knee of the pictured pianist.

"Damn fool!" Steven cried.

Except for the idling motor of the truck, everything went quiet for a time. The silence was broken by a cacophony of sharp, explosive cracks. Behind the stacked bales, Gretta lay very quietly with her head and heart pounding. She gradually worked the stuffed rag out of her mouth with her tongue. She sensed movement from Howard's direction, but thankfully he too remained quiet.

"Throw what's left of the painting in back and let's go. You didn't touch anything else, did you?" Steven asked as he looked at the two dead bodies.

"No. Besides, I have my gloves on," Steven's partner replied in broken English with a thick Spanish accent.

"It'll be hours before anyone finds these two imbeciles," Steven said, not knowing that Gretta and Howard were lying on the other side of the rotting hay.

A sliding door and two additional doors slammed shut, and the truck engine revved. Gears ground as an inexperienced driver pulled the truck out of the old barn and gathered speed. The odor of exhaust fumes drifted through the barn, and all was still. Gretta lay still while quietly spitting the remainder of the filthy rag from her mouth. A hand pulled at her tied wrist, and she tried to jerk it away.

"Take it easy. It's me," Howard whispered. "Are you hurt?"

"Oh, Howard, I'm so sorry ... so sorry!"

"For what? I think we surprised some thugs fencing some art."

"How did you get loose?" Gretta asked.

"The nitwits tied my wrists to rotten beams. I'm surprised you didn't hear me breathing heavy as I tried to pull free. I finally did."

Gretta looked up into the face of her husband of six years and saw the deep concern in his eyes. As she lay there in pain, she thought, *what a fool I've been!*

After untying her, Howard smiled lovingly down at his wife and brushed the bridge of her nose with the back of his forefinger, hand as warm as his smile. "Think you can walk? We should try to get back to the car and wait. Sooner or later, somebody will come along and give us some help if our car hasn't been spotted already."

Together they climbed out of the rotting hay and spied the two dead men. Not recognizing either one, Howard and Gretta gingerly stepped around them.

"The police will have to sort this out," Howard said as they walked through the already open barn door. The eastern sky was just beginning to show the light of morning as they stepped out. There was a chill in the air, and everything was wet from the night's rain.

As the two started to walk away from the barn, Howard turned to look at it one final time and said, "We sure know how to pick them, don't we?"

He didn't realize the double meaning of his statement, but it felt like a dagger to Gretta. What he'd unwittingly said rammed the point home. She too had some real sorting of her own to do, and there wasn't much time to do it in. How much should she tell Howard? How much should she tell the police? And how in hell was she to tell Steven to fuck off? Gretta wondered whether the police could privately help her without having Howard learn the whole story. Perhaps she could still save her marriage. She decided to answer the next call from Steven after she had privately talked to the police. Pandora's box had to be closed regardless of the price.

WHICH SHIP?

A massive blast of a horn made Oliver flinch slightly as he gazed out his cabin window at the Statue of Liberty as it lazily slipped by. He turned his attention to the brochures of his ship, the *Olympic*. There was various instructional material in the stack on what to do and not to do during the voyage. Accompanying the brochures was the evening menu for first class stamped with today's date, April 13, 1912. He tugged at his starched collar and removed it. It was three, and he had been wearing that collar since six this morning, having come from an early meeting at the New York office of the Pinkerton Detective Agency for a final briefing prior to his trip.

There was a knock on his door. "Mr. Livermoor, are you in?"

He walked to the door and looked through the peephole. An attractive woman, slender and about his height, greeted his eyes. He guessed her to be in her early to mid-thirties. She wore her hair long and flowing over her shoulders. She was not an attendant.

"Yes, can I help you?" he responded as he opened the door.

"Please forgive the intrusion. I discovered you were sailing alone, as I am, and I wanted to know if you would like to join me at the captain's dinner tonight? It is a semiformal occasion, and I would really appreciate an escort."

"Quite frankly, Miss ..."

"Alice Miller."

"Quite frankly, Miss Miller, that's one of the best offers I've had all day! Please step in, and I'll fix you something to drink. To what do I owe this unexpected pleasure?"

As he led her to a captain's chair, he noticed that the once-cozy compartment seemed to have dropped some in temperature. The brochures on the convenience table rustled a bit and exposed a brief on the *Titanic*. It was a bit odd, but perhaps the parent company displayed the two ships in the same brochure bundle since they were sister ships from the same cruise line.

Sitting down in the offered chair, Alice said, "I know I dropped in on you a bit unexpectedly, but an evening out would mean a lot to me right now."

"Well, Miss Miller, your company is a pleasant surprise nonetheless. Until you came along, I was anticipating a boring dinner with a lone drink in my hand, endlessly stirring it."

"It's agreed then," she said, looking up into his eyes.

He took her hands and helped her to her feet, momentarily shocked at how cold her hands were.

Noticing his awareness, she said jokingly, "Cold hands, but a warm heart."

He chuckled and then said, "Wait a minute, I was going to fix you a drink!"

"No, that's okay! I see it's already a little after three. The dinner is at seven. How about I stop by your compartment later, say around five thirty, and we can go to the bar and spend a little time together before having to go to the gathering?"

"That sounds good to me. Let me accompany you back to your room."

"That won't be necessary, Mr. Livermoor. It's just down the hall. I'll pick you up around five thirty, okay?"

"It's your show, dear lady."

With that, he watched her walk down the long corridor, and when she was out of sight, he stepped back into his room and closed the door.

Wait a minute, he thought, *at least get her room number.* He opened the door to call after her, but there was no one to call out to. He muttered to himself, "If she disappeared that fast, her room can't be very far away! At least she's close by, in the vicinity anyway."

Sitting at the bar with drinks in their hands, she turned and looked directly into his eyes once more. "I'm grateful for this favor, more than you possibly realize. Someday I'll repay the kindness." She reached out with her glass and clinked his.

"You're absolutely stunning this evening. If you don't mind, I hope to see more of you. That is, if I'm not being too forward."

"You're not, but let's enjoy the moment. We no longer have the past and don't really know what the future holds, at least most of the time anyway. All we have is the present, a fleeting moment."

He smiled. "That's pretty profound, but I have to agree with you."

"Not to change the subject, but what is your line of work, Mr. Livermoor?"

"Please ... call me, Oliver, and may I call you by your first name?"

Smiling, she said, "Fair enough ...Oliver."

"Well, my work is with the Pinkerton Detective Agency, founded in the 1800s and headquartered in Washington. I work out of the New York office. So, basically, I'm a detective."

"Now, if I'm not being too forward, what brings you to this boat?" she asked.

He laughed. "Well, I'm on my way to meet my counterpart from Interpol, in Cherbourg."

"It sounds like exciting work."

"It can be at times, but at other times it's quite tedious. Okay...now tell me something about your life."

"Is this an interrogation?" she laughed. After a pause, she said, "Well, I have one vice for sure, and that is genealogy. I can really get lost in it."

"Interesting! I must admit I'm intrigued."

The dinner bell rang, calling everyone from the bar and their respective conversations, drawing their attention to the dining area. The plate stewards were moving about through the private groups, asking them to please take their seats, so that everyone would be seated before the captain arrived.

She looked at him and said, "Come; let's go. I'll tell you more about myself later."

"Is that a promise?"

"It's a promise."

She brushed his cheek with her hand as they got up to go to their appointed seats. Her fingers were cool against the hot skin of his face. Chilled from her drink, no doubt. She was becoming more and more of a mystery. He had to admonish himself not to play the role of detective for at least one night.

The dinner itself was more entertaining than he expected. Her companionship undoubtedly played a key role in his enjoyment. Aside from the dining festivities, Oliver did pick up on something the captain said during his brief speech: that the ice floes in the North Atlantic were at an all-time high. But the passengers were not to worry. The captain reminded them that the *Olympic* and her sister ship, the *Titanic*, were unsinkable. He added that the crew, however, would be extra vigilant in watching for any ice that might come their way. The captain ended his speech on an up note by reminding them that they were in good, capable hands. He encouraged them to relax and enjoy the voyage.

Oliver suggested to Alice that they take a short after-dinner walk along the open promenade deck before retiring to their respective cabins. She agreed to go if it was to be only a short walk. The sky was full of stars, and the breeze was soft. It was a Sunday evening, and Oliver felt the most relaxed he had been in a long time. However, Alice seemed to be tense. When he took her cold hand in his, he noticed that she was trembling.

"Is something wrong?"

"What time is it?" she asked.

"Well, it's now about eleven thirty-five. The night is still young."

"No! No, it's not!" she exclaimed. "We must be getting back to our rooms! My father will be waiting for me!"

Well, that might be the explanation for her vagueness, for some of it anyway. "Can I at least walk you back to your room?"

"No, that won't be necessary. I'll be all right. I'll see you tomorrow!"

She pulled her cool and clammy hand out of his and dashed off into the nearest entryway, which opened to a long corridor.

"Wait, you're headed the wrong way!" he called out, sprinting after her, but to no avail. "Disappeared again," he said after halting and catching his breath. First thing in the morning he would check with the registrar's office and see exactly which cabin was hers.

That's what I should have done in the first place, he thought. "Some detective you are!" he mumbled.

At eight thirty the next morning, he found the registrar's office several floors below his compartment level. He started to speak but then noticed the fearful and ashen faces of the staff members.

"Is something wrong?" he asked.

"That's an understatement," the clerk said with tears in his eyes.

"What happened?" Oliver asked.

They all turned and looked at him, and the clerk asked, "You don't know?"

Now Oliver was getting a bit edgy. "Don't know what?"

The clerk responded, "Our sister ship, the *Titanic*, sank roughly four hundred miles south of the Grand Banks of Newfoundland shortly before midnight last night."

"You've got to be kidding! These ships are supposed to be unsinkable! How could such a thing happen?" Oliver asked.

"An iceberg! A damn iceberg took the big ship down!" The clerk started to cry and quickly left the room.

A fellow staffer explained to him that the clerk had friends on board the downed ship.

"How many survivors?" Oliver asked in a hushed tone.

"Not many, I'm afraid! It's estimated between fifteen and eighteen hundred perished."

"Good grief!" uttered Oliver. He had to sit down.

One of the staffers walked over and put a hand on his shoulder. "When you came in here, did you have a question?"

He took a moment to clear his head. "Yes, yes I did. Could you please tell me the cabin number for a Miss Alice Miller? I believe her cabin is near mine, cabin A29."

The head clerk perused the guest list and shook his head. "No, we don't have anyone listed under that name. Are you sure you have the right name?"

"Yes, reasonably sure. She said that was her name. She was traveling with her father. Could you look for a Mr. Miller?"

"Perhaps you misunderstood me, Mr. Livermoor. Though Miller is a common last name, there are no Millers on our guest list, period."

After pondering a moment, he pulled out his badge. "Would you mind then if I do a little quiet investigating on my own? I would like to interview some of my fellow passengers, both to the right and left of my compartment. You can assign an attendant to accompany me in this if you wish. We may or may not have a missing-person situation."

The head of the registrar's office said, after inspecting the badge, "I don't see a problem in that. I'll clear it with the captain just to make sure, though, and get back to you."

"That would be fine, and thank you for listening to me under these circumstances." Oliver took his leave and went back to his cabin.

There was a message waiting for him from the onboard Marconi wireless operator's office asking him to disembark at the scheduled stop in Queenstown, Ireland. From there he was to backtrack to either Newfoundland or Nova Scotia depending on where the investigation into the *Titanic*'s sinking would be conducted. He was to offer Pinkerton's help and assistance in the investigation. A purse to cover his expenses would be waiting for him at the harbor master's office in Queenstown. This had all the earmarks of a publicity stunt capitalizing on a catastrophe. He was told not to worry about making the connection in

Cherbourg. Another Pinkerton representative would be stepping in to take his place.

"Change of plans. What a mess!" Oliver muttered.

He sat down at the highly polished convenience table and thumbed through the brochures once more. To his bewilderment, however, there wasn't a single piece of *Titanic* literature included in the stack. He remembered a *Titanic* brochure being there when Alice had first come to his room. Now she and the *Titanic* flyer were missing.

What is going on?

Something told him he would not have any luck in interviewing any of his fellow passengers. His past twenty-five years in the service of Pinkerton had taught him the law of cause and effect didn't always hold up. Over time he had discovered some very shocking conclusions when ultimately there was no other answer. Upon further reflection, he was anxious now to get to Queenstown. He would go through with the interviewing of his cabin neighbors but had little confidence in the outcome.

It took a few days to backtrack to Halifax, Nova Scotia, from Queenstown on a Cunard liner. The recovered bodies and what debris existed were being collected in Halifax, along with what information could be gleaned from the survivors. Upon arrival, Oliver reported to the port authorities as a member of the Pinkerton Detective Agency and volunteered his services. However, he was basically told, "Thanks, but

no thanks." They did say, though, they would get in touch with him if they felt his help was needed. They dutifully recorded where he was staying. As far as his front office was concerned, he'd done what he'd been asked to do. He had time now to work on his own agenda, using his hotel room as a base of operations.

Using his badge, he obtained copies of the three lists that had been compiled in the port authority office in Halifax: those who had been rescued, those whose bodies had been retrieved and who had been pronounced dead, and those who were still missing and by now presumed dead with no hope of retrieval. Examining these lists seemed like a good place to start.

Not sure exactly what he hoped to glean from his examination, Oliver first scanned the list of the rescued, which availed him nothing. However, in the second list, one thing did jump out at him. It appeared first-class passengers had been preferentially treated. Even the owner of the ship had managed to find a lifeboat when literally hundreds couldn't.

His mind wandered a moment. *Was my fling with Alice just my imagination? Or if she was telling the truth about her name, was she a stowaway?*

After a short break, he started to peruse the third list. He got down to the *M*S, and there appeared the name Alice Louisa Miller!

"No ... how could it be?"

He continued to read. Alice was thirty-six and assigned to first-class cabin A29 with ticket number 1753. Her last residence was New York City.

What is going on?

She had the same cabin number as his on the

sister ship *Olympic*! He jotted down the information and went to the nearest telegraph office. He needed a favor from his front office in New York. He wanted them to track her down and get any information they could. He stressed the importance of this request for him personally and promised he would make up the expense himself. Depending on what information they could dig up, there was every bit a chance that this Alice Louisa wasn't the same Alice he'd met.

He waited forty-eight hours before returning to the telegraph office. The forty-eight hours of pacing, walking, and wondering were starting to take their toll. There was a reply waiting for him. It affirmed she was a resident of New York City and single. It also affirmed that she was a member of the Colonial Dames of America and had a keen interest in genealogical studies. It turned out she was a descendant of Andrew Hamilton, one of the more renowned colonial lawyers.

Oliver cabled back a thank-you to his New York office and returned to his hotel room. He tried to sort things out. It would be difficult to share his experience with her with anyone else. To him, their time together had been very real. He'd had an enjoyable dinner date with a lovely, sophisticated lady, mirage or no mirage.

A soft female voice came from the shadows in the corner of his room. "Yes, Oliver, for us and us alone our time together was very real. I can't tell you how important it was for me. I'll be waiting to return the favor for you one day. But this time, when I take your hand once again, it won't be cold; I promise."

He could feel her smile.

"Goodbye for now. The years ahead of you will pass quickly." With that she spoke no more and disappeared.

The reference to her cold hands proved to Oliver more than anything else that she was the right Alice. He had found her. Somehow, in some way, two lives had overlapped by the strangest of commonalities, entwining them.

ABOUT THE AUTHOR

Tristan Armstrong is a military veteran who worked in industrial research. Now retired, he is the co-author of two novellas, Boudica's War and Carcassonne under Siege. When he is not writing, he expresses himself artistically through layered digital imaging.